Fortune's Folly

by

Barbara Jean Miller

Fortune's Folly

Cover Art by *The Wild Rose Press, Inc.*

The Wild Rose Press, Inc.
PO Box 708
Adams Basin, NY 14410-0708
Visit us at www.thewildrosepress.com

Publishing History
First Edition, 2024
Trade Paperback ISBN 978-1-5092-5383-8
Digital ISBN 978-1-5092-5384-5

Published in the United States of America

Dedication

For all my substack newsletter followers

Chapter One

"Aunt Agatha says I may come to London." Roxanne Whitcomb sat still for a moment at the small desk in their sitting room as she waited to see if her brother Fredrick had heard her, but so far she could see only the his curly brown hair as he bent over his plans. She cleared her throat, shook her dark curls, and repeated herself more loudly.

Fredrick finally looked up from the drawings that covered their dining table. "What was that?"

"Aunt Agatha says I may come. I can stay with her and search for an investor to partner with you on your steam engine design."

He smiled sadly and shook his head. "Rox, that is not what she expects you are coming for. She thinks you've finally agreed to her bringing you out so that she can marry you off."

"It may come to that." Roxanne could not imagine leaving Fredrick to his own devices. He would forget to eat.

He got up and came to lean over her chair and tug on one of her curls. "I don't want you selling yourself to some jaded man of the ton just so you can convince him to fund my inventions."

"What else am I to do with myself?" She looked

1

around the neat-as-a-pin room that served all their needs. The upstairs bedrooms and back kitchen also shone with an early morning cleaning. Only the kitchen garden might miss her attentive hand, and Cook could hire a boy to help with that.

"Keeping house for me should not be your life's work either. Do you mind so much we've had to lease the estate to Captain Vance and take up residence here in the gatekeeper's cottage?"

"I mind that he married Mother only a year after Father's death. What was the point of leasing the estate out if he plans to live in London and Paris? We never get to see Mother."

"At least we have a bit of money coming in," Fredrick said. "In truth, I think Father's friend only leased the place to give us an income. He's the executor and must know our affairs are in a bad way. Besides, it's easier to keep up this cottage, and the empty stable provides space for my workshop and forge."

Roxanne cringed at the mention of the stable. It was indeed empty, all the horses having been sold at auction at their guardian's orders. That meant nothing to Fredrick, but it had hurt Roxanne, who loved to ride. "It can't be so that Mother would have the house she is used to. They are never there."

Fredrick went to poke at the fire. "It was a bit of a shock, her marrying him. Shows the state of her desperation."

"She didn't have to do it to provide for herself. We could have taken care of her. I'm sure she doesn't love him."

"You can't know her mind."

"I know she was a strong woman, before, and

passionately in love with Father."

"Even a strong person can be broken by a suicide and the loss of everything."

Roxanne flung her pen down. "She didn't lose everything. She had us, but she just left for London, then married him without even telling us ahead of time. It wasn't like her."

"They have been away," he said to the fireplace. "You haven't even seen them together. Perhaps she has come to love Vance."

Roxanne watched him mend the fire better than she could. "I suspect love seldom enters into marriage."

He turned to her. "I have no idea, but this is all so different from the life you were meant to lead."

"I like it here. I have a purpose, helping you with your work and reminding you to eat. I'll leave Cook with instructions to annoy you until you do eat your dinner."

"I'm trying to say I don't want you to make a loveless marriage, not for my sake."

"I'm disillusioned with marriage. I don't care if I find a husband or not."

"You're disillusioned with Mother's marriage. Perhaps I should come with you. London isn't the safest place in the world."

"Neither is Exeter, and I go there by myself in the pony trap all the time."

"Don't remind me. Can't Cook do the marketing?" He hung the poker back on the stand.

"I shall be fine. Aunt Agatha would never let any harm come to me in London. Besides you will be coming for your birthday anyway. There will be papers to sign when you come of age."

"I suspect I will be inheriting a mountain of debt, but

I will come."

"All the more reason to find you an investor. Now I must write an answer to her and pack my best clothes." She turned to the small desk she used for correspondence and got out a piece of parchment.

"Don't remind me. I should take better care of you. It's just that I get involved in my work." He pulled out his pocket watch and checked the time. "I know. I can take you shopping before you go."

Roxanne laughed. "I'm not leaving this minute. Besides, you know whatever we buy here will never be fashionable enough for her." Roxanne stood and stroked her worn buff work skirt. "She will toss it out and buy me new."

"Which is why I do not like to visit her often. I don't like her spending her money on us. It makes me feel cheap."

"But it's not as though I want for anything. I think we go on quite well." She hugged her brother.

"Spending all our money on my work. You would." He kissed her cheek and stood back to look at her.

"I would rather get a job and support myself," Roxanne taunted.

He shook his head. "It simply isn't done."

"It's done by most of the women I know, including Cook."

"But not by a genteel lady."

"I am barely a lady and certainly not that genteel."

"Not when you are ranting at the tradesmen for trying to cheat us. You have a scary reputation locally." Fredrick gravitated back toward the table and his plans.

"I am glad for it. I will not let anyone take advantage of us, but we must get your inventions funded. That is why leaning on Aunt Agatha is necessary. We can pay her back when you are rich and famous." She leaned on the end of the table, looking at the latest changes to his design.

"I was wondering why we don't just ask Aunt Agatha to invest in my high-pressure steam engine."

Rox laughed. "Can you imagine trying to explain it to her? And she'd never agree."

"But if you are to fake husband hunting, is it not possible you will find yourself in a position where you must accept someone?"

"I may have to make that sacrifice if it is required of me."

Her brother looked pained. "I don't want you to sacrifice yourself for me."

"Fredrick, since I have not fallen in love with anyone in all these years, it seems unlikely I am romantic. A marriage of convenience might suit me very well."

"But is this fair to Aunt, you pretending to comply with her wishes while you keep your own agenda?"

"I can do both. I will be at my most subtle."

Fredrick tried to rub the worry lines out of his forehead. "Rox, you are always frank to a fault and never subtle."

"I can be clever as well."

Fredrick leaned on a chair at the table, making it creak. "What I mean is that I wish you would find someone, a husband. I don't mean for his money, but someone who would take care of you better than I can."

Her brother really did care about her more than his inventions. She had to think of a way to allay his fears.

"It's a big city. The season is at its height. With a

little good fortune I might just manage both. Now go back to work while I answer this letter."

She hoped she sounded enthusiastic about a trip to London. She would never tell her brother that need was the only thing that would force her into the ton again. Her only romance, if she could call it such, ended with their father's death when her fiancé dropped her.

She would never trust a man again. But this was different. She would be the predator in this case, someone who took advantage and got enough financing to help her brother with his work. No other solution came to her other than to trade her life for his happiness. If they did not move quickly, someone else would a build a high-pressure steam engine and get the patent before Fredrick.

Chapter Two

Two weeks later, Roxanne was working her way around the edge of an elegant candlelit ballroom, scrutinizing the men and feeling not quite so predatory. She realized now that she had no notion how to go about entrancing a man, even one she didn't care about. They looked at her, some even with interest, but those were sure to be the ones her aunt warned her away from. How on earth could you tell a respectable man from a gamester or fortune hunter? They all had gleams in their eyes.

Due to her inattention, she brushed elbows with a younger girl in a white dress who was hurrying from the room.

"Are you unwell?" Roxanne spun to pursue the girl.

"No, I am fine."

"But you are crying," Roxanne whispered.

"Take no notice. This always happens. They don't like me, you see." The girl paused to regard her. "You are looking for someone. Who?"

"A cit, and a wealthy one."

The girls fair brow wrinkled in concentration but her tears stopped. "My brother is a cit, but I don't think you should use that term."

Roxanne followed the girl into the hall. "A business man? Really?" Perhaps he would be a candidate."

"But 'cit' is a term of disparagement." She looked

worried, but for Roxanne's sake.

"Have I offended you, then? I only wanted to find someone to invest in my brother's steam engine designs. Has your brother investments in mines?"

"I don't think so. Our fortune came from wool manufacturing, but lately it's the foundry that Spencer is most interested in."

"That's no good. I need someone who owns mines."

"You came to London just to find an investor for your brother? Why didn't he come himself?"

"Too modest. He has talent and brains but no ambition. Actually, my aunt is bringing me out to find me a husband."

"I'm Holly Tanner, and I am looking for a husband as well, rather against my will," she said. She wrenched open the double doors of a room at the end of the corridor and led Roxanne inside.

"I'm Roxanne Whitcomb."

"Yes, I know."

Roxanne stared up at row upon row of volumes, more than she could ever read. They'd had a library like this at Whitcomb Hall until it had been put to auction. She craned her neck to look around at a room bigger than her whole cottage, and spun to admire so much literature, her cream silk evening gown swirling about her. And this was just Mr. Tanner's town house. What must his country estate be like?

She stopped herself. She could not possibly prey on Holly's brother now that she had struck up an acquaintance with her. She would far rather have Holly for a friend and confidante than Spencer Tanner for a husband.

"So neither of us really want to marry. It's

comforting somehow to know that I'm not singular in that respect. Friends?" She stopped and waited for Holly to compose herself. The girl looked to be a few years younger than her, which awakened Roxanne's sympathy.

"I have never had a friend before."

"Am I too bold to call you 'friend' already?"

"No, but what have the two of us in common if you are only looking for an investor and I am avoiding the prospect of marriage?"

"Dear, Holly! I have no designs on your brother. I like you for your sweet self. We just seem somewhat alike in not knowing how to play this game."

"And not even wanting to." Holly moved nervously about the room, which said something for her agitation because it was a restful room. "Friends, by all means, for I sorely need a confidante."

Roxanne followed Holly with her gaze, trying to calm her by example and distract her. "Do you think your brother might know anyone who owns a mine?"

Her new friend stopped and stared at her. "I can ask. For now, I must hide from these people for a few moments." She retreated behind a sofa which was pointed toward the fireplace.

"Who are you hiding from? Who doesn't like you?"

"Any of the girls also searching for husbands. They resent that I have a large fortune and may snag someone they want."

Roxanne sat down next to her. "When really you would never want to marry someone who only cared about money."

"Exactly, because he would be like Spencer or worse. Only concerned about money. I know my brother cares about me, but sometimes he's so cold, and he just doesn't listen to me. Roxanne, you are Lady Sherbourne's niece, aren't you?"

"How do you know that?"

"From the receiving line. Don't you recall? I was in it. This is my brother's house."

"I'm so sorry. I have a horrible memory for names. My head spins every time I meet a group of people. When my aunt quizzes me about them later, I never get them straight."

"You don't seem like the others."

"Arrogant, you mean? Frivolous? I have no reason to be, but I am angry that someone insulted you in your own house. You should tell your brother."

"Oh, no, I must not, for he has a terrible temper and might ruin all. Spencer thinks I am having a wonderful time. The ball is for me, so I can't be complaining about the guests. If he gets angry, he might do something rash."

"He should do something rash if they are rude! Your brother should throw them out. And if you don't like them or want to get married, why not anger him and put an end to it?"

"Oh, you are too much like him." Holly almost cringed. "Please promise me you will say nothing to him about those girls."

"Of course not, if you don't wish it."

"So little is in my control, I thank you for that. I have my duty to Mother to think of. I could never embarrass her."

"Shall we go out together so you don't have to fear these predatory misses? I will stare them down for you."

"I don't think you should. Then they will gossip about you as well."

"People always gossip about me. Why should London be any different?"

The door opened and Roxanne turned her head to watch a tall, well-dressed man enter. He had blond hair, fashionably cut, but his handsome ordinary face was lent character by a scar over one eyebrow. He had something else, a sort of presence, a solidity like a stone wall. She had the feeling she could lean on him and he would never buckle.

Then Roxanne remembered him from the receiving line. Only then his smile had been artificial and now it was genuine. She could tell in an instant that he truly did love his sister. That put him out of bounds. If he was a good man, there was no way she could take advantage of him.

"I thought I might find you here. Who is your companion?"

Roxanne smiled and stood up. "I am happy I am not the only one to mislay names. I'm Roxanne Whitcomb."

He approached with a broad grin. She offered her hand, and he took it lightly. Then she realized the action was probably forward of her, especially when he gazed at her as though memorizing her face.

"It's the eyes," she said. "No one can decide if they are green or blue."

He grinned again and dropped her hand. "Sorry if I was staring. You are Agatha Sherbourne's niece. There are so many to remember."

"And you are Spencer Tanner. At least I have that right. We are discussing if Holly would be allowed to come to tea tomorrow. We are only a few streets away, on Manchester Square. And her mother, as well, if she wishes to come."

She glanced at her new acquaintance and saw the girl's eyes open wide in amazement. What was so startling about a polite prevarication? She would have invited them to tea, given a bit more time.

"If they'd like. I will bring them myself."

"You are invited as well, of course."

"I will bring Holly. Mother does not go out much, though I will ask her. For now, there is dancing going on, and you are both missing it."

He led them back to the ballroom, one on each arm.

"Who is your partner for this dance?" he asked Holly.

"I don't have one."

"You should dance with your sister, Mr. Tanner, so she sees how it is done."

"Very well, and then may I have the next dance with you?"

Roxanne went through the formality of checking her empty dance card and said, "It's open." She was sure he realized her ruse, for he smiled again when he left her.

As Roxanne watched brother and sister perform the country dance, she racked her brain to remember anything Aunt Agatha had said about the Tanners. It was something to the effect of, "We may as well use the invitation. Everyone will be there. But they are in trade, my dear, and only one generation removed from the mill. Perhaps not even that. It is said that Tanner supervises his own businesses."

She had better forget about Spencer Tanner even though she admired a good worker. It struck Roxanne as particularly difficult to tell if a man had money or not. They all dressed in finery and looked wealthy, but her aunt had warned her away from one or two men who had been noticing her. Though she was as good at evasion as stalking, what was the point? Eventually she would have to dance with someone to assess his suitability as an investor.

When Tanner came for her, she felt her forced smile turn genuine. Finally she could relax for a few moments except for minding the steps of the dance. She did not have to worry about Tanner's motives. He was just being polite. But did she have to monitor her own? He was wealthy, apparently, but she could never use a spontaneous connection to his sister to stalk him, even as an investor.

In the few moments of the dance when they were together, he asked after her relations. She told him about Fredrick and his high-pressure steam engine design as a matter of course. How could she not? After all, he had asked. But it was difficult to deliver a proper description of such a device when interrupted by the movements of the dance again and again. It was worse than trying to carry on a conversation while riding horseback with someone.

As he led her back to Aunt Agatha, he asked if he could take her in to supper.

"But your mother should sit with you."

"She has gone upstairs for the night. All this is too tiring for her."

"I hope she feels well enough to come tomorrow."

"So do I." Tanner nodded to Agatha and smiled at both of them.

"I would be delighted to have supper with you."

He went off then to cajole a young man into dancing with Holly.

Aunt Agatha raised an eyebrow at her and fluttered

her fan. "I see you have attracted the attention of Mr. Tanner."

"You say that like an accusation." She smiled at her gray-haired aunt to take any sting out of the remark.

"He will do if we cannot find a title for you, but we have only just begun."

"What is wrong with Spencer Tanner? He seems approachable and honest, unlike so many if these men."

"I told you—no title, and his money comes from the factory. Mind you, only dance once with any of them."

"Even Mr. Tanner?"

"He is the host, so he may claim a second dance with you."

"Seems to me a title isn't much use without money."

"And you shall have both. You will rescue the family integrity. Once we have you married, we will see what we can do for your brother."

Roxanne stepped back a pace when she considered this possibility. Perhaps her childless aunt was using them to fulfill her ambitions. "I don't think Fredrick would like that."

"Nonsense. Once you've brought the family back to respectability, Fredrick will need a wife and heirs."

It was worse than Roxanne had realized. She was supposed to puff herself off as some sort of paragon who would make everyone forget her father's disgrace. She could almost guarantee that wasn't going to happen. In fact, the reverse was far more likely, for she did have a temper.

In her moment of inattention, her aunt almost sprinted across the room to collar an older gentleman. Now she was glaring at Roxanne, who didn't know what to do. The stiff, graying gentleman was the last man she wanted to dance with. Finally, Agatha came over to grab her arm. The man trailed slowly after her.

"I want you to meet Sir John Marbrey," she whispered. "I know a knighthood is not much of a title, but it's a start."

"He looks so old and sad."

"I'm sure he's quite charming. Sir John is also very rich."

"Well, I shall be careful not to offend him, then, but I see now that trying to describe a high-pressure steam engine to someone on a dance floor is not practical. I shall have to make a later appointment with him."

She left her aunt gaping as she walked toward Sir John. Roxanne tried to smile as she closed the distance between them, but her face felt frozen as her aunt scampered up beside her to made introductions.

"I am not much of a dancer," Sir John confessed, "but I would like to lead you in to supper."

"Oh, dear, I am most honored but I already promised someone else—our host, in fact. I did especially want to make your acquaintance." She bit the side of her mouth over that lie. Still, perhaps he was a potential investor. Older men did such things.

"Perhaps I could take you for a drive tomorrow. I have a fine new team."

"A drive would be lovely. Any time before tea. The Tanners are coming tomorrow."

"The Tanners are coming to tea tomorrow?" her aunt asked.

"I should have asked your permission first. It was an impulse."

"Of course, that is fine. Perhaps Sir John would also like to come."

"I shall call at one o'clock for the drive, and stay to tea. What a splendid plan."

As the older man walked away, her aunt stared at her.

"You know Tanner is one of the wealthier men in London. And suddenly he is leading you in to supper and coming to tea tomorrow. How did you manage that?"

"I struck up a friendship with his sister. She is very nice. In fact she is the only girl who has spoken to me tonight."

"Very clever of you, Roxanne."

"I wasn't trying to be clever. I like Holly."

"Inviting them to tea is fine, but you don't want to sit in Tanner's pocket, at least not yet."

"But I have an assignation for tomorrow. Many more people will notice me with Sir John than with Tanner."

"True, but tonight they will see you being singled out by Tanner."

"Hmm, perhaps I should continue to mingle." Roxanne scanned the edges of the ballroom, but all those not dancing were gathered into gossipy clusters. The chances of singling out such a man as she was looking for seemed slim. Probably he would be a husband or otherwise ineligible.

"I think you should stay by me so I can find you partners."

Before she could answer, a naval officer bore down on them and bowed to her aunt in a dashing manner that overwhelmed the older woman.

"You may not recall me, Miss Whitcomb. Captain Harding. I am in the shore guard, the Preventives stationed in Exeter. Actually, we are now known as the

Coast Guard."

"I thought you looked familiar. This is Lady Sherbourne, my aunt."

"How do you do, Captain Harding?" her aunt asked with a nod.

"Very well, Lady Sherbourne. And yourself?"

"If you are in the shore patrol, what brings you to London?" Agatha asked.

Roxanne felt her aunt was as good as turning him down.

"Refitting my ship."

"What a happy circumstance to bring you here," Roxanne babbled. The Preventive officer, who had once warned a seaman away from her on the quay in Exeter, was a welcome relief, but she hoped he would not mention the incident to her aunt. "It's so nice to encounter a friendly face among all these strangers."

"I am surprised you recognized me, since we have never before been introduced. May I stand up with you for the next dance?"

Roxanne opened her mouth, but her aunt intervened. "The next dance is a waltz and she is not permitted."

"What a shame. Then some refreshments, and we can bring lemonade back for Lady Sherbourne." Captain Harding took Roxanne's arm and walked her toward the blue salon.

As Captain Harding led her away, she looked back over her shoulder and could see Aunt Agatha was still gasping much like a hooked fish.

"As neat a cutting-out operation as I have ever seen," she remarked with a grin.

Harding's black brows drew together over his lively brown eyes. "Where did you learn naval cant?"

"My brother spends a deal of time in the harbor, and I shop in Exeter."

"So you knew what I was up to and let me lead you away." He scanned the salon, which was just as noisy and crowded as the ballroom.

"I have been cautioned not to make a scene."

"And you are not at all impressed by the uniform?"

"A uniform is always pleasing. Have you any interest in high-pressure steam engines?"

"What on earth are you talking about?" He looked at her as if confronting a lunatic.

"I thought not. We seem to have little in common other than your gallant rescue of me in Exeter."

"Normally, I admire snap judgments."

"When they are correct?" she countered.

"When they are mine," he said. He led her toward a table that looked to have safe beverages. "You are the oddest sort of girl."

"So I have been told at length and frequently." She stopped at his elbow.

He smiled at her reply. "May I call on you tomorrow?"

"Tomorrow I am engaged all day."

"Ah, the lemonade. Here, hold this for your aunt. Or would you rather try champagne?"

"I would rather know your mission."

"That's blunt."

"I have no conversation, but I must warn you I also have no fortune, so if you are looking for a rich wife, alas, you must continue the operation." Roxanne scanned the room as though to hunt out possible prey for him.

He laughed. "And yet I feel I want to know you better."

"Why?" She had done her best to dispel any illusions he might have.

He shook his head. "I have no idea, really."

Roxanne opened her mouth to put him in his place but realized she enjoyed arguing with him, and there was something else. He was bold, and she sensed he might lend courage to a girl who had not enough of her own. A girl like Holly.

"Please come to tea tomorrow, 16 Manchester Square."

"Very well. What will await me there? Court martial? Keel-hauling?"

"A pleasant surprise, I assure you."

"Miss Whitcomb." Tanner came toward her. "It's nearly time for supper."

"Ah, Mr. Tanner. You found me."

Harding relieved her of the lemonade. "I shall take this to your aunt and see if she has a partner for supper."

"Captain Harding, that is most kind of you."

"Wish me luck," he said with a nod to Tanner.

She stared after him wondering whether luck would mean he did escort her aunt or if he did not.

"As it happens, I shall escort both you and Holly to supper." Tanner frowned as he said it, but only for a moment.

"Oh, I can't believe no one else asked her. How could they all be so rude in your own house? Perhaps Captain Harding would do."

He patted the hand she had laid on his arm and looked speculatively around the ballroom. "We can't make them like us. I should not have said that, since I realize you are one of them."

She chuckled. "Mr. Tanner, I will never be one of

them. Holly feels lonely at these events not knowing any of these people."

"She is waiting near the dining room. She is far too shy for her age."

"Better a becoming shyness than the forwardness I see displayed by many of these girls." Roxanne snapped her mouth shut, then laughed. "I can't believe I said that. I sound just like Aunt Agatha."

Tanner gazed down at her with merriment in his eyes as Roxanne inwardly upbraided herself. If she were more socially adroit she would have been able to throw Holly and Harding together for supper, though she had noticed a twitch to Tanner's mouth when she had mentioned Harding. Patience was a virtue she seldom practiced, but it might be wise to attempt it now.

"True. Your aunt is typical of the society matrons."

"Perhaps I should include myself among the too-forward misses."

"I would never think so."

"But I steal a march by criticizing myself, so that you feel compelled to deny the truth."

He chuckled. "How long have you been playing this game?"

"Not long enough. I am only used to jousting with my brother."

"So this is your come-out season?"

"Yes, crone that I am. I dare not tell you my age."

"You cannot be much above Holly in age. You won't manage it again."

"What?" She had truly lost track of the exchange.

"Trick a compliment out of me."

"A challenge. I shall make it my mission. There she is."

"I do wish at least one of these young men had asked for her hand."

"For a dance, perhaps, but not for life. None of them are worthy of her, save perhaps one."

"Which one?"

"I don't think I'll tell you. Not just yet."

****

Tanner guessed she was only joking, so he dropped the subject and led them into the room where a table had been set aside for them. He thought that if Roxanne was an arrogant sort she'd feel happy to be sharing supper with him, but she only looked nervous. Was he showing her too much preferment, or was she embarrassed to be seen to be the focus of his attentions, cit that he was? Generally, he did not read people accurately but took them at face value. Miss Whitcomb was the first person he had met tonight who seemed genuine. Yet she claimed to have found out the one man who would be worthy of Holly. He just wished he had her divining rod, for he had begun to think this whole season was a terrible mistake.

He had learned a little of society in his stint at school and university. If people envied you, they could cause you a deal of trouble, and you would never know what was coming until it landed on you unawares. He hoped that Miss Whitcomb's only concern was that she attracted his attention when he had denied it to the three predatory mothers and daughters who had been trying to trap him tonight. Would she suffer their gossip because of his actions?

He couldn't change public opinion. But he could court this bold and strangely disquieting girl. That was not all he could do. He could possibly scare other suitors away from her. So he had better make sure he did not ruin her chances with others unless he was certain he was willing to offer for her.

How fast his mind leaped toward marriage, when it had been only an idle thought before the season started. But he had just met the one woman whose wit and humor made London exciting. Perhaps that was not enough to induce him to ask for her hand, but he meant to pursue an acquaintance with her.

He smiled at her as his servants uncorked champagne for them. His father had wanted him to marry into the ton to further their business interests, but his father was dead now, and Tanner saw no need for such an alliance. He had built the family fortune to the point where he no longer courted investors.

For the first time he realized how much freedom he had. He *could* marry Miss Whitcomb. She got along well with Holly, and she didn't turn a cold eye on him like some of the other beauties, who had accepted his invitations but apparently only to meet their friends.

Spencer was sure Holly was embarrassed by not having a supper partner, but what could he do? Without his mother's support and her society contacts, he could not force any of these men to care about his sister as he did. Why his mother was not more supportive of his efforts to find Holly a husband he was not sure. His sister needed a future in society instead of being caught between two worlds.

The two girls chatted during the light meal, and he realized how charming and animated Miss Whitcomb was, talking about her father's estate near Exeter. It was called Whitcomb Hall. Oddly, she mixed tales of hunts and house parties with advice on how to grow the best cabbages and the future importance of high-pressure steam engines to industry. At the end of half an hour, his head was spinning but pleasantly so, and Holly was enthralled.

There was more dancing after supper and more young men to find to dance with Holly. But he did notice now that if she stayed by the vivacious Miss Whitcomb she got some partners on her own. Spencer didn't like the look of all of them and apparently neither did Miss Whitcomb, for she seemed to draw off the older or more dangerous-looking men for herself.

Tanner saw the naval officer who had just danced with Holly approach Miss Whitcomb again, and there was nothing he could do. He had already danced twice with her. Who made that stupid rule anyway? But the officer did not look avaricious. Simply glad to see her. And they conversed easily. How could he compete with such familiarity? They must know each other. Plus he had a uniform. Tanner wondered why his mother had invited the young officer.

Naval service was dangerous even without a war. So this man must appear much more of a hero to Roxanne than a cit ever could. Tanner had never felt jealous of another man's occupation before. Perhaps it was how Roxanne smiled at the other man and chatted to him without effort.

Tanner realized he wasn't jealous of the uniform but of anyone else capturing Roxanne's attention in such a way. No woman had made him feel like this before, and he wasn't sure he liked it or himself for not controlling his possessiveness. He had better bridle his jealousy before their next meeting or his temper would get him into trouble.

"Captain Harding. Still looking for that dance?"

Roxanne asked.

"You seem to be making a hit."

"I feel like a fish out of water, but my aunt is sponsoring me, so I must feign having a good time."

"May I have a dance now?" He bowed formally.

"It will be a wonderful relief to dance with someone who will not interrogate me."

Harding glanced around the room. "Are they so bad?"

"Only the ones who don't know the family history. For the others, I should wear a sign that says, *No fortune*."

"Ah, yes, your father's untimely death. You would think they would forget in, what is it? Three years?"

"Gossip has a life of its own."

"As I find while I am stuck in London waiting for them to refit my cutter. My sister brought me as a guest, so I am a bit of a sham."

"I am as well."

"Yet I hear from Miss Tanner you got them to come to tea tomorrow. That's a coup."

"Is it? I just wanted Miss Tanner to feel more comfortable in London."

"Even though you don't."

"Perhaps we can share our discomfort with the situation."

"I shall be delighted to attend, even though your aunt is glaring at me as though I am some sort of upstart. I asked her in to supper and she glared at me, but I must have been the best offer she got. Talk about interrogation."

"About what?"

"*Your* life in Exeter, not mine. It was difficult to

convince her I enjoy only a nodding acquaintance."

"Pay no attention to Aunt Agatha. She's hunting a title for me."

"And not a military one, I wager. I wish her well. You deserve an easier life than the one you've had."

She looked up at him. "So everyone around Exeter knows."

"They are probably more sympathetic than the *ton*. Forgive me for bringing it up."

"It's good to know what they are saying of me. Sometimes I almost catch it, but the girls break off with a titter."

Harding's brow furrowed. "It's not your fault."

"Yes, it is. I decided to come here."

"Then face the whirlwind." Harding laughed. "You are proof against it."

"Sometimes I wonder if it's worth the bother."

"But you are a hit among the men."

"You are the only one with a serious thought in your head, and in your case it's not about high-pressure steam engines."

"What?" His dark brows came together in confusion again.

Roxanne could see that she should at least explain why she was here. Captain Harding might even be able to put her in the way of some investors. So she launched into her speech and kept his attention for a good quarter hour. He actually understood the uses of such an invention. Why did all the intelligent people not have any of the money?

How unfortunate that she could discourse with Harding for hours as though he were another brother, but with Tanner she had to guard her words. She did not want him to think her predatory. It would be wonderful to have someone so rich interested in her brother, yet it could not be because Tanner felt sorry for her.

Much as she enjoyed the company of the clever Harding, she would have preferred to spend her time with the thoughtful and stolid Tanner. Harding was all on the surface, a hero for the working day. Tanner had something deeper that could only be released by the right woman. She just wasn't sure she could be that woman.

****

In the small hours after the ball, Tanner lounged in the chair behind the large desk in his study. He was drinking a brandy and not enjoying it much, for he wasn't sure what to do next. Invitations for his mother and Holly had been sparse before. This ball was to have launched his sister, yet it seemed to him as though his mother had withdrawn her support of his campaign to find a husband for Holly. Perhaps she realized he was using his sister as a stalking-horse so he could find a wife for himself.

He was not sure what he would do if a flood of invitations did not arrive on the morrow. Perhaps the whole idea had been a terrible mistake. Except for Miss Whitcomb. He would never have foregone that experience.

He never knew what Roxanne was thinking and had no idea what she would say next. She was no governess-trained miss, mouthing commonplaces in the hope of pleasing him. She didn't seem impressed by his wealth and showed no signs of being on the hunt for him. It was Holly she'd invited to tea. If that was subterfuge it was clever, but he did not think Roxanne was capable of intrigue. And he had every intention of escorting his mother and sister to this tea tomorrow.

It wasn't just that Holly seemed more outgoing now. Miss Whitcomb attracted people to her. Perhaps she and her aunt could get his sister some invitations to houses he had been unable to breach, where people would be nicer to her. That seemed like using them, of course, and he hated the notion.

There was also the attraction of seeing Miss Whitcomb again. But her beauty was not her only feature. Her conversation was startling. He did not mind it was sprinkled with facts about her brother's inventions, for she seemed to know her stuff. It was that she always spoke frankly and confided in him, perhaps more than she should in a new acquaintance, though he had no notion of betraying any confidence she might tell him.

There was something indefinable that attracted him to her. Roxanne Whitcomb was a puzzle to him and he would never be able to keep away from her until he figured out what drew him. He enjoyed the complete openness of her conversation. It made him feel as though he had known her a lifetime.

He realized that if they married he would be able to come home from the foundry and tell her about his work. She would understand what he was talking about in a way Holly and his mother never would. He tossed off the rest of the brandy and made his way up the stairs toward his chamber. He had a hundred things to do at the foundry, but he was actually looking forward to this tea more than he had anticipated anything in a long while.

He loved his work because it was complicated enough to engage his whole mind. Perhaps that was it. Roxanne Whitcomb was complicated.

Chapter Three

Roxanne found the drive with Sir John less than satisfactory. He talked of nothing but his son and heir and his daughter-in-law, who ran his households both in London and in the country. Roxanne could see that marriage to him would result in nothing but battles, and that these self-same relatives would discourage their father from any worthwhile investments. Besides, his new team was a pair of her father's horses. She could only think of the last time he had taken her driving. She could hardly tell her escort the reason for her somber mood, but she didn't think he noticed.

He talked of his properties and blessedly did not question her except to inquire about her accomplishments. She assured him she had none. She neither played nor sang, and she stank at watercolors.

"You must have some skills."

"I ride with the best of them, and I'm a fair shot but only at targets. I hate to shoot birds."

He chuckled at these revelations, but it was a relief when they finally arrived at Manchester Square so entertaining him was not solely her responsibility.

She had worried the cook into agreeing to a host of pastries and was not disappointed when she returned and saw the tea table which had been set up in the morning room.

She and Sir John had barely seated themselves when

Captain Harding arrived. Roxanne could see her aunt's scowl of disapproval at receiving a man who was not a prospect. She could not tell her aunt why she had asked him to come. He was amusing and kind, and Roxanne had simply thought that if someone was going to marry Holly for her money he may as well be handsome and hardworking. At the very least, Harding would put Holly at her ease.

To Roxanne's delight, Spencer Tanner brought both his mother and sister and said he had time to stay for tea. Mrs. Tanner and Aunt Augusta embraced and kissed, to the surprise of nearly everyone.

"How many years has it been?" Agatha asked.

"Since our season. Nearly thirty. I should have written more."

"I should have answered more."

"I'm so glad you accepted the invitation to Holly's ball."

"It was not just for Roxanne's sake. I wanted to see you again, but I lost my nerve after I met you in the receiving line. I'm so glad Roxanne invited you."

Roxanne cast Spencer a questioning look as he led his mother to a chair, and he shrugged. She enjoyed this secret communication between them.

"I had no idea you two were acquainted before," he said.

His mother sighed. "It was a long time ago, and we promise not to bore all of you with reminiscences."

"Let us instead speak of the balls to come," Agatha said. "My ball for Roxanne will be Friday. I hope you, all of you, will be able to come." She clearly included Harding in this sweep.

Roxanne thought this was not just because Harding

looked dashing on the dance floor. When Holly had come in, Roxanne had surrendered to her friend the seat by the captain. She saw her aunt's calculating look, and suddenly Harding was on the approved list since Aunt Agatha perceived what Roxanne was about.

"I would enjoy it above all things," Holly said. "Not to be the center of attention will be less stressful."

Lady Agatha looked surprised. "Most young ladies enjoy being the main attraction." She began pouring the cups of tea and passing them around as the maid offered the tier plate of cakes to each person.

"Not me. I had rather watch the dancing than dance."

Harding smiled. "But you dance very well. And so does Miss Whitcomb."

Roxanne laughed. "I have not stepped on you yet, at any rate. If Fredrick were here, he would warn you."

"Fredrick?" Tanner asked.

"My brother and only dancing partner, up until two weeks ago. Aunt hired a dancing master to sharpen my skills."

"And you claimed your only talents were riding and shooting," Sir John teased.

"Roxanne," her aunt lamented.

"Shooting?" Tanner inquired.

"Father taught us all at the same time. He thought it was something a soldier's children and wife should know how to do."

Harding nodded. "The state of crime being what it is, I think it a useful skill."

"Will your brother come for your ball?" Holly asked.

"I'm not sure he can pry himself from his work."

Tanner stirred his tea. "That's right. You said he is working on a design for a compact steam engine."

"Yes, a high-pressure steam engine."

Agatha cleared her throat. "Perhaps we should not have Fredrick here. All his talk of steam engines and pressure vessels makes my head spin."

"They say someday soon ships will be powered by steam engines." Captain Harding winked at Roxanne.

Tanner nodded. "Yes, and wagons to haul the coal the new ships will need. It would be easy to find oneself obsolete."

"Better to ride the wave than be crushed by it," Harding said, popping a bite of scone into his mouth.

"Then you both agree Fredrick's work is important." Roxanne couldn't believe how smoothly Tanner had introduced the topic. Now she could not be blamed at all.

"If what you described last night is possible, a better casting for higher steam pressure, then his work could lead the way to smaller engines, useful in more applications."

Roxanne felt herself positively beaming at Tanner. Not only might he help her brother, but it had been his idea. That was the sort of hero she wanted, a man who could make such decisions. She couldn't be happier if he had asked her to marry him.

She was aware of her suddenly warm cheeks. Perhaps that offer, if it ever happened, would eclipse this one. But how to get there was a puzzle. She had discovered at the ball that she had no arts or wiles for attracting men.

"Could we not speak of something more entertaining?" Sir John asked.

With that, her hopes of him as an investor were

completely dashed, but there was still Tanner.

Tanner smiled. "Sorry to let business intrude."

Captain Harding nodded. "Yes, we should plan some entertainments for our disdainful maidens. I fancy there are some things in London you both would like. An evening at Vauxhall?"

"A play opening?" Tanner suggested.

"Perhaps a drive to Kensington Gardens," Sir John put in.

"Yes," Holly said. "I should love all those things."

"We have a theater box at the Agora," added Tanner. "Why don't we all go tonight?"

"May Captain Harding and Sir John come?" Roxanne asked.

Tanner smiled. "Certainly."

"And I shall get us a box at Vauxhall," Harding said. "We will go there by boat. I can make those arrangements."

"Suddenly London does not seem so frightening." Holly smiled at all of them.

Roxanne had never felt so much a part of a group before. She'd been only sixteen when her father died. Before that, she had experienced only rowdy country balls. She hadn't minded being isolated with her brother for three years, but she now knew she had missed something without realizing the lack of it. Friendship.

"Make all the plans you wish, but remember to save Friday for our ball," her aunt added.

Sir John stood. "I shall be honored, dear lady. For now, I must not keep my horses standing any longer. Perhaps I shall see you at the theater. I have a box at the Agora, as well, in case we need more chairs." He bowed over Roxanne's hand last.

After he left, Roxanne bit her lip. "I hope we didn't offend him."

In spite of this comment, Harding looked less than concerned about the well-being of Sir John. "He offered to drive to Kensington, so he is throwing himself into our plans to entertain you. Besides, we may need his box for the play."

Aunt Agatha glared at Roxanne. "When he said he had a box as well, that was an invitation for you to sit with him, Roxanne."

"I did realize that at the time. I thought only that it would be improper."

Her aunt frowned. "His son and daughter-in-law will be there, of course, providing a good chance for you to meet them."

"But I've already heard his whole life story. In fact he began repeating himself, so I can't think conversation in his box will be at all lively."

"Still, if he asks you tonight, you should go sit with them."

"Very well, but I fear people will read too much into such an action, and I hope he realizes that."

Tanner frowned. "I'm not adept at society signals, but it seems to me it would be bad form to accept an invitation to my box, then take a *better* offer later."

"Got you there, Aunt Agatha. I'll stay in Tanner's box."

Tanner wanted her to sit with him. That meant he was interested in her as more than a friend for his sister. When she contrasted what her evening would be like with Tanner as opposed to Sir John, she felt a bubble of excitement rise in her. Tanner would not talk over the lines of the actors. When he spoke he would say clever things to her. He would think every word she uttered was witty. The evening would be perfect.

****

"Do you like the play?" Tanner whispered to Holly. He could see that Roxanne's attention was rapt, but Holly had been fidgeting and now whispered to him behind her fan.

"Yes, but even when the actors are speaking, people keep staring at me and whispering over the lines of dialogue."

It was true. He could see faces dip behind fans in the red-and-gold-glowing theater, and men bobbed their heads to listen. Spencer thought he caught the words *ten thousand a year* more than once. How could these people know what his sister's income would be?

"They are admiring both of you, the two brightest stars in the theater."

Roxanne chuckled and whispered, "A joint compliment and skillfully delivered, but I do wish the lights were dimmer so we might focus on the actors."

Harding glanced around them. "We may be the only ones who wish to watch the play or hear it. Ah, we are coming to the end of the act and may walk about during the intermission."

Holly shook her head. "How am I to bear this falseness I perceive about folk in the *ton*? No one means what they say, and all they care about are themselves."

Spencer looked at Roxanne and noticed her troubled brow. It was not so bad for Holly, who had him to protect her interests, but for girls like Roxanne who had no choice but to sell themselves for a fortune, the prospect must be daunting. He often thought the women who worked in his weaving factory were better off. At least they had their freedom of choice.

"Playacting perhaps is a necessity sometimes," Roxanne said, "but to put yourself before others seems to me impossible."

Tanner had a sudden remembrance of Roxanne's kindness to Holly. "Because you never do it, Miss Whitcomb. You always think of others first, even boring old Sir John."

"I see many around me much worse off, so I do not worry overmuch about my own fate. Besides, so many things can surprise you and founder the best-made plans."

"One must be willing to take risks," Captain Harding said.

"But not on a throw of the dice," Tanner agreed. "Only an honest risk where there is some chance of success."

He smiled at Roxanne, but she was looking pale and hurt. What had he said to wound her so?

"Would you like something to drink, Miss Whitcomb?" Harding extended his hand toward her, and she took it for support as she rose. "Perhaps some lemonade?" he asked.

"Yes, above all things, Captain Harding," she whispered. "I shall go with you, and we will carry some back for the others."

Tanner watched them exit through the curtains and wished he had been the one to take Roxanne for lemonade. There was something amiss, and he needed to ask her what.

He turned to his sister. "Holly, if Miss Whitcomb is feeling unwell, we could leave."

"She did not say so, but she looks unlike herself. I

shall ask her when they return."

"Was it something I said?" Tanner squeezed Holly's hand.

"How could you possibly discomfort her?"

****

Roxanne was glad of Captain Harding's arm as they made their way through the crush to the place where they could buy refreshments.

"Here, drink this. It will bring your color back." Harding placed the glass in her hand.

"He's right, you know. The daughter of a gambler, moreover a speculator, one who lost close to everything in the stock market."

"Tanner never listens to society gossip. Be assured he had no idea what he said would pain you so."

"But I am here under false pretenses, to try to get funding for my brother's inventions. I did not think to…"

"To what?"

"Deceive anyone. I must get through this ball my aunt is hosting, then perhaps back to Exeter and my small life. At least that is honest."

"A captain of the coastal guard is not on the same level as a captain of industry, but I have a house in Exeter and a small estate from my father. If all else fails—but I see by your face you must have Tanner."

She felt herself blush, then shook her head. "No, I know now that I must not entertain an offer from either you or him or I would play us all false. Nor can I marry another under false pretenses. How odd that this false place has shown me some truth about myself."

"At least realize he did not mean to hurt you."

"I should hope not. I have been betrayed by both parents and had thought my brother my only ally."

He took her free hand and warmed it inside his. "If ever you could bear to marry for comfort, for a love that is only mine and not yours, I remain your loyal servant."

Roxanne freed herself and patted his arm. "You should never marry out of duty or some misplaced sense of gallantry. I see you watching Holly, the pure innocent, the one you could actually fall in love with. She needs someone like you, a guide and protector, someone who would treasure her for herself, not her wealth."

Harding shook his head. "I do not aspire to her hand. Besides, I just asked you to marry me. I should not now be talking of another woman."

"You should not be talking nonsense. Captain Harding, if you were to marry someone who didn't love you, you would regret it for the rest of your life."

"You would feel the same if you were to make a match for reasons other than love."

"You mean money. I am used to disappointment and sacrifice. I'm used to the idea of not having a future. If only I can make things easier for Fredrick. I am willing to marry without love so long as the man doesn't love me either."

"I suspect your brother might find your abject devotion and self-sacrifice misplaced as well. Did you ever discuss it with him?"

"Yes, and you are correct in your opinion of him, but his work is important." She finished her lemonade and took the glass she meant to carry to Holly.

Harding shook his head. "So is your happiness."

"I have been so long unhappy, I'm not sure I could handle happiness at this late date."

Spencer wanted to go to Miss Whitcomb to find out what had discomposed her so, but he could not leave his sister. He saw Sir John watching the box from across the way and even wondered if the man's gaze had upset her.

Miss Whitcomb was quiet for the rest of the performance but had regained her poise by the time they braved the crush of people to get to his carriage.

"What is on the agenda for tomorrow?" he asked.

"Shopping in the morning, then Vauxhall Gardens at night," Holly answered. "What time shall we come for you, Roxanne?"

"Whenever it is convenient."

"Ten o'clock, then, and mother has invited you and your aunt to luncheon."

"I'm sure Aunt Agatha will be delighted. I know they wish to talk more."

Tanner observed Roxanne until they delivered her to her aunt's door. She seemed so lifeless compared to her usual vivacity.

"Are you indeed well?" he asked as he gave her his arm up the steps.

"I am perfectly fine. But Holly is right about society and wise for someone so young. You are going to have to be careful, Tanner, that she is not preyed upon by a man who doesn't really care about her."

"You face the same danger."

"No, the dangers I face are entirely different. Good night."

He went back to the carriage stunned by her parting words. What possible danger could Miss Whitcomb be in? His puzzlement must have shone in his face.

"What is it, Spencer?"

"Is there something I don't know about Miss Whitcomb? She seems to think she is in some kind of danger."

Holly thought before she answered, her sweet face puzzled in the faint lamplight that occasionally shone through the window as the carriage moved through the streets. "She took her father's death badly, and her mother absconded to Europe, by what I can make out. She has only her brother and aunt left to her. London is scary enough for someone like me, with all the servants who guard me."

"I don't think that's what she meant, that she was afraid to go about in town."

"She feels she must marry to support her brother's inventions if she cannot find an investor. I would dislike it terribly if she had to barter herself in such a way. Do you think you might be interested?"

"In fact, I am."

"Good, then you can invest in Fredrick's machines and Roxanne won't have to marry. She doesn't really want to."

Tanner mentally staggered at this misinterpretation of his intent. "Oh, I see." He didn't know much about women, but he guessed this would be a bad moment to declare that he wanted to marry Miss Whitcomb, not just invest in her brother's plans. How could he have read Roxanne so incorrectly? She had seemed genuinely interested in him.

But what Holly had just told him smacked of servants' gossip. What if she was wrong and Miss Whitcomb did wish to marry? He had best not close any doors until he had a genuine talk with either her or her brother. How was it done when the father was dead? He would at least wait for the brother to appear.

Chapter Four

The next day, Roxanne recalled that she should prepare for a shopping expedition. As she poured hot water into her flowered wash basin, she decided it was rather dreary having Aunt Agatha buy things for her. She would much rather use up her small store of coins than be forever dependent on a relative who told each store clerk to send her the bill. Her aunt seemed delighted to be showing her off. Otherwise Roxanne's conscience would not allow so much charity.

After she dressed in another new walking dress, this one of mint-green muslin, she went downstairs anticipating some hot tea.

Aunt Agatha's butler Greeves sent Roxanne a warning look as she placed her hand on the knob to the morning room.

"What?"

"Captain Vance and his cousin have called."

"Oh, no. That's all I need. What is he doing in London?"

"They did not say, miss."

"Are they alone?" she whispered.

"Lady Sherbourne is with them."

"A coward would grab her pelisse and run to the lending library."

Greeves inclined his head as though giving her permission. "Shall I call a footman to escort you?"

"No, I am no coward, and I shall have to confront him sooner or later." She wrenched open the door and went in.

"Ah, Roxanne. I believe you have not met my cousin Ian Stone."

"No. I did not recall you having a cousin." She curtsied and Stone took her hand roughly and kissed it. He did not resemble his cousin much. But that was to his advantage. He was not oily and snakelike, but rough and desperate-looking, his smile nervous and his eyes anxious. Roxanne could relate to him being ill at ease. He must not have sold out of the army as Vance had, since Stone still wore the scarlet uniform of a dragoon. Probably on half-pay.

"Your aunt tells me you make an expedition to Vauxhall Gardens tonight?" Vance asked.

Roxanne realized she had been staring at Stone, so she swung back to Lucius Vance and seated herself beside her aunt. "Yes. Is my mother in town?"

"Yes, she needed to consult with her physician."

"I had thought you were fixed at Paris. Are there no physicians there?"

During her interrogation she noted that Stone seated himself and did not take his gaze off her.

"Come now. It is only a few days by carriage and a short trip in my yacht. Did you think we would not hear of your come-out?"

"We saw no need to write," Aunt Agatha said. "Besides, I think your presence will only remind people of the gossip we had hoped would die down."

Vance laughed unpleasantly. "If you think three years is enough for the *ton* to forget a suicide, you are naïve. Now answer my question, Roxanne."

"I am going to Vauxhall with a few friends." She was beginning to feel unnerved by Stone's gaze. "Is Mother at the town house?"

"Yes. You should call on her."

"I shall." She was determined not to let him get the better of her.

"When she is feeling better," Vance added, his eyelids drooping over his snake-like gaze.

"Tomorrow, perhaps. If you only just arrived, she will need time to get settled."

"She will be well enough for your ball."

"What is wrong with her?"

"Nothing serious. We were surprised to hear of your come-out. We thought…" He paused theatrically.

"Yes?" She refused to finish his sentence for him.

"We thought perhaps it was too early for such a move."

"Fredrick is nearly of age. The lease on the estate is almost up. He will be getting on with his life and so must I."

"I suppose the die is cast, so we may as well make the best of it." He turned to his cousin. "I'd like Stone to accompany you tonight. Just for your own protection."

Roxanne blinked at the mention of dice. "Are you telling me Vauxhall Gardens is dangerous?"

"Only to your reputation. And you must be very careful with yours."

"That's hardly my fault. I have been very careful, though I can't help thinking your arrival may bring up past memories for everyone."

"My arrival?" He placed one hand on his chest as though nothing could be his fault.

She stared back at him. "I mean with Mother."

"She wants to see you. It's been two years since we left London."

"I am of Mr. Tanner's party, to which Stone has not been invited. However, if we meet there by chance, I do not think Spencer Tanner would take it amiss for you to join us." She turned to Stone but did not smile at him.

He grinned. "What time should I *encounter* you?"

"We are going by boat. We should be there by seven."

"Ah, taking the water route," he said in his husky voice. "Sorry to miss that part of it."

They were scarcely out the door before Roxanne drew a sheet of paper toward her and penned a note to her mother. It was difficult to know what to say after three years.

She could not possibly convey any of her aunt's reservations about their appearance in London. In fact, she did her best to make her mother feel welcome even though she'd had no word from her in all this time. She had written to her as long as she'd had an address—that was until they had left England. After that, there had been no way to contact her. The question that remained in Roxanne's mind was why her loving mother had not sent her word, not even a small note of explanation, as to why she had married Vance.

Roxanne still loved her mother, but time and distance had made her feel abandoned. She tried to defend their mother to Fredrick, who attributed the marriage to grief and weakness. But until Roxanne talked to her, she could not know. Just because Roxanne could not figure out a reason for the marriage did not mean there was not a good one.

Seeing Vance again and hearing the way he referred

to the S*ilverloo* as *his* yacht, Roxanne began to ponder more sinister motives for her mother's capitulation. Did Vance hold something over her head?

None of that could go into her note of welcome. Often the weighty issues of life could never be openly discussed because it was too much like opening a wound. Instead, a fog of small talk cast a veneer of normalcy over the most awful situations. She was not satisfied with what she'd penned, but it would have to do. She rang for the footman rather than carrying it round herself, then braced for a tiring day of shopping.

****

Roxanne found boating to Vauxhall charming. Part of her delight was sitting beside Tanner as Harding stood in the back of the skiff giving directions to the oarsmen. It brought back memories of her father's yacht, the *Silverloo*, and what wonderful sails they used to take out of Exeter. She had thought herself the luckiest girl alive. Since she loved sailing so much, she wondered why she wasn't more attracted to Harding, who made his life at sea. But Tanner was more of a mystery. She sensed something burning inside him. She just did not know what it was.

Mrs. Tanner had agreed to chaperon the girls. This seemed both wonderful and frightening to Roxanne, who worried that the health of Holly's mother might not be up to the expedition. Then she recalled that Holly's mother was Tanner's responsibility, so she was able to breathe easier. He would not have let her come if there was any danger. And he could take care of her in any event.

Roxanne could not say why she had such ultimate confidence in him, but he seemed aware in a way her brother was not. Tanner did not need her nurturing. That meant he could take care of Roxanne for a change…if that was what she wanted.

She enjoyed Harding's narration of their journey as they were rowed along the river. The lantern swinging on its pole lent a holiday feel to the trip. And the seats were not damp, as Aunt Agatha had feared, but were covered with cushions.

Perhaps she was enjoying herself because Captain Harding seemed so confident and Tanner trusted him. The two men were on the way to being friends, as far as she could see. That would fit into her plans for Holly and Harding.

They arrived without mishap and took their seats in the alcove Harding had bespoke, to enjoy the concert. Roxanne managed to sit beside Tanner with his mother on the other side. That meant Holly and Harding were seated next to each other. Her aim had been to throw them together. But to feel Tanner's strong presence beside her was comforting and exciting at the same time.

She had not realized before how she went about mentally armed to ward off gossip and insult. Harding was correct in that Tanner had no intention of hurting her. Roxanne now felt safe with Tanner beside her.

He excited her beyond what she thought possible, and she did not know why. Perhaps it was his potential to do or say the unexpected. He was like a large bomb, and she did not know what would ignite his fuse.

A break in the music gave Stone his opening, and he approached the box. Reluctantly, she introduced him. As Roxanne had predicted, Tanner raised no more than an eyebrow about the inclusion of a soldier to the party. Stone stayed with them through the light supper, though he drank rather than ate.

When Holly wished to stroll the grounds, Stone suggested the four of them should go together for propriety. Tanner stayed to entertain his mother. When she saw his qualms about being left out, she volunteered to stay with his mother in his place.

"But you will miss seeing the gardens," Stone said. He took her hand in a compelling grasp and raised her to her feet.

"Just don't get lost," Tanner warned.

Roxanne did not see how this could be possible with so many lanterns and so much of the vegetation planted in rows, but she nodded her agreement.

Though he had a long stride, Stone reduced his pace to let the other couple draw ahead, laying his hand over Roxanne's small one on his sleeve. Roxanne thought it was unwise to fall behind, yet made no objection, to give Harding an opportunity to talk to Holly in private. She wanted to make sure they did not get out of sight, or Tanner might complain of her not watching Holly.

"You don't find the music romantic?" Stone asked.

"I'm not a schoolroom miss, entranced by music or beautiful gardens or even a blood-red uniform. Why does your cousin want to throw you at my head?"

He twitched his head sideways to stare at her. "That's frank. I suppose he wants you to marry someone, and he doesn't think you will find anyone in London."

"He doesn't know Aunt Agatha."

"So who do you plan to marry? You have to get Vance's permission, you know."

Roxanne stared warily at him. "No, I have to get Mother's permission."

"Do you forget that Vance is your guardian?"

"Since I haven't seen much of his guardianship, yes,

I did forget."

"He thought taking your mother away would scotch the scandal."

"Of my father's death, or her second marriage?"

She caught the snort of laughter from him. He seemed armed for any attack she might make against him.

"You don't understand how it was during the war. Friends in the army always took care of the survivors. Many a soldier married his friend's widow within the week, to offer her protection."

"In case you have not noticed, the war is over. In fact it was over long before Vance married my mother."

"Lucius did wait a year. Why are you so angry at him?"

"I'm not sure. I suppose he reminds me of the very worst day of my life."

"Three years. You should be over that by now."

She replayed the shot in her mind. It was the sort of noise that your dream state tried to find an explanation for in the moment before you awoke, but she had known right away something fatal had happened. Running downstairs to the library, pounding on the door, hearing Vance say she must not see this, then going to get her mother. The servants would have stormed the library had not Vance finally opened the door. "It's as though it happened yesterday."

That got his attention. He gazed at her intently, and one hank of brown hair fell across his brow in a desperate way. "Just remember I am here for you."

"I'd have trouble forgetting that, since I seem chained to you."

He dropped her hand. "I am not your guard."

"You're not?" Perhaps he was insensitive just because he was a soldier.

"I am, in a manner of speaking, but I have your interests at heart. If we were to marry, I could take care of you." He swaggered as he said this with one hand on his sword hilt.

"It is not every woman's ambition to be cared for."

"What, you don't want to live at a great estate and be the lady you were meant to be?"

"What great estate?" She stared at him, since he hardly looked prosperous.

"Whitcomb Hall. Lucius said I shall be the manager."

That stopped her, but seeing Holly and Harding make a turn ahead of them impelled her forward. "That would be up to my brother."

"True, but would he deny me the position if we were married?"

"Probably not. He doesn't pay much attention to estate matters. I was always allowed to run his household."

"Then there is no impediment." He pulled her off the main walk under a trellis with benches beneath it.

The aroma of roses was oppressive. She tried to wrench free, but he seized her by the shoulders and tried to kiss her. He would have succeeded except she managed to clip his jaw with the heel of one hand. Her tiny blow scarcely knocked his head aside, and he laughed.

"You beast! Never try that again."

"Do you forget?" He tightened his hold. "You marry me or no one."

"Then no one."

Roxanne was still trying to kick him in the knees when he was hit and carried away by a large dark body. The two men landed on the bench and smashed it. At first she thought it was Captain Harding, but then she recognized Tanner's blond hair in the bars of moonlight that pierced the screen of trees. Her heart gave a surge of pure joy. She had known she could count on Harding, but to be rescued by Tanner was above anything she'd expected.

And Tanner seemed to be getting the best of Stone in spite of the other man being a soldier. Still, she picked up one the wooden arms of the bench, just in case he would need her assistance.

Harding ran up then, with Holly on his heels. "Cease and desist! Recall where you are, gentlemen." Harding laid a restraining hand on Tanner.

"Stone is hardly a gentleman." Tanner rose and let the other man up. Stone was bleeding at the nose, she noted with satisfaction, and Tanner was scarcely out of breath.

"I think you should leave, Lieutenant Stone," Harding suggested.

As he blotted his face, he glowered at Roxanne. "You just remember what I said."

"Yes, it relieves my mind not to have that worry any longer. I shall simply refer all candidates for my hand to your cousin. That should keep him busy during his stay in London. I'm sure he'll thank you for that."

"What was that about?" Harding asked as Stone strode off.

"He tried to kiss me." She handed Tanner her handkerchief to blot his split lip.

Harding shook his head. "God help any man who

tried to do more than that."

Roxanne laughed, and Holly gave a gasp that turned into a giggle.

Tanner brushed off his clothes and looked at her. "Why are you holding that club?"

"In case he should escape you." She still felt the need to club Stone but didn't want Tanner to think she doubted him.

Harding started laughing and could not stop.

Holly went to examine her brother's face. "Are you sure you are all right, Spencer?"

"Of course, but we had better leave before word of this gets out. And Miss Whitcomb, put down that piece of wood, if you don't mind. You should have known I could handle him myself."

"It wasn't that I doubted you. I'm simply not used to being kissed—or rescued from it, for that matter."

Tanner blew out a tired breath. "I can see that. Now walk sedately with me to Mother."

"Oh, goodness, is she sitting alone?" Roxanne tossed the lumber aside and took his proffered arm.

He smoothed his waistcoat so calmly with his free hand she could hardly credit he'd just won a brawl. Tanner wasn't even breathing hard.

"No, your aunt came after all, by carriage."

"What great good fortune. Otherwise you would not have sought us, and I would have had to deal with Stone alone."

His head snapped sideways to stare at her. "Do you think you could have?"

"I'm not sure, for it never occurred to me I might need to carry a weapon in London."

Harding started laughing again. She realized Tanner

was staring at her, and he was not smiling.

"Well I do generally carry a pistol when I drive to Exeter. Perhaps I need one here as well."

"Was this one of the dangers you spoke of?" Tanner whispered urgently.

"No this is one of those events that come up on your blind side."

Tanner escorted Roxanne to a seat beside her aunt and checked her appearance. She did not look at all like a damsel who had just been accosted and had armed herself with a cudgel. Her nerves were not overset, and she chatted to her aunt about the gardens as though she had been having a wonderful time. Harding was still chuckling to himself when Tanner asked if he should perhaps arrange for their return boat.

"Oh I brought my carriage," Lady Sherbourne said. "Did you not see the fog creeping in? I think we should all ride home together, not that I fear your safety on the Thames with Captain Harding in your boat. Now tell me what has really happened. Roxanne is babbling, and she never does, so something is amiss."

Tanner cleared his throat, but Roxanne launched into a description of the fight that gave him more credit than he was due. A gentleman would have challenged Stone and met him with pistols, but he had started a brawl like a schoolboy. Still, it had felt good to be able to do something in her favor, even if it was destructive. If anyone had seen them, the gossips would have a field day tomorrow.

"Did anyone witness this disagreement?" Lady Sherbourne asked.

"Only Miss Tanner and myself," Harding said, "and you know we will say nothing."

"Then we need not be too hasty in leaving, through Mr. Tanner could use a cold cloth on that lip."

He blotted it again with the edge of Roxanne's handkerchief and promised himself that he would buy her a dozen to replace it. How had he slipped into thinking of her by her first name? He had not won her by his show of outrage on her behalf. He glanced at his mother to see how she would take this upset, and she was smiling at him. Now what could that possibly mean? She should be shocked. He was shocked himself that he had completely lost control and dived at Stone like an opponent in a wrestling match. But there was just something about Roxanne that brought out the worst in him.

Not the worst, perhaps, but what he really felt like doing and saying. She did not stand on ceremony, so he did not feel he could either, when he was around her. He wanted to tell her the truth about everything, specifically what he was feeling for her.

What held him back was not the possibility of his failure as a suitor. Her aunt wanted a title and fortune for her. He could supply only the latter, but he was used to buying everything he wanted. He was sure Lady Sherbourne had a price. What worried him was that he did not feel worthy of Roxanne. She had been willing, even expecting, to have to defend herself after he foolishly let her walk off on Stone's arm.

What happened tonight was his fault, and he was fortunate that Roxanne was not the sort of woman to fall into a swoon or the vapors. She had more courage than he could rightly expect in a woman. His wish right now was to take care of her for the rest of her life.

But Roxanne's love could never be bought. He was

going to have to earn it. Dispatching one annoying suitor was not enough, in his book, to deserve her. He must think of something else.

On the way home in the carriage, he relived the moment when he had seen Roxanne in danger. He had not stopped to think at all but had launched himself at Ian Stone with murder in his heart. He tried to tell himself that he would have felt the same way if any woman was in danger, but he knew that was not true. There was something about Roxanne Whitcomb that touched his heart. She was nothing like Holly, yet she needed him— or he wanted her to need him.

Ostensibly the London season was for Holly, but he had toyed with the notion of meeting a sensible, amiable women to act as his hostess. Roxanne was nothing like the bride he'd been contemplating, and yet she had something. He just wasn't sure it was something he could handle.

Still, she had befriended his sister and mother when no one else seemed inclined to include them. And the two older women knew each other. That was a plus and had seemed to draw their party together nicely with the addition of Sir John for dignity and Captain Harding for levity. Tanner found himself actually anticipating their next expedition, but it was Roxanne whom he dwelt on most in his reverie. He seriously never knew what she might say next, and that was her attraction.

Chapter Five

Roxanne sent another note to the their town house early in the morning to see when it would be convenient to call on her mother but had received no reply by the time they all took a quick luncheon in the breakfast parlor. The servants were busy with ball preparations, and Roxanne found herself dreading the evening more than she had anticipated. She'd told her aunt what Stone had said about Vance needing to approve her husband. Agatha merely said they would wait until her brother was of age. Certainly Vance's guardianship would pass to Fredrick at that point. Roxanne was far from certain of anything at the moment.

The agonizing hours of preparation crept by, and the only bit of anticipation she could look forward to was seeing Tanner again. Harding and Holly as well. But Tanner was her hero now, a man of action who didn't care the snap of his fingers for conventions when she was in danger.

As they stood in the receiving line, a line of only two, Roxanne wondered where her errant brother was. It would have been comforting to have him beside her even if he was distracted by thoughts of his inventions.

Holly and Tanner arrived early, soon followed by Captain Harding, so she did not feel so very alone after that. But she once again had terrifying lapses of memory and stopped saying, *So happy to meet you*, switching to the safer, S*o glad you could come*. She had met many of these people before, but she simply could not connect them to their names.

The leering misses she had rather not remember. The crush was nothing like Holly's ball, but there were enough people to wrack her nerves. Then she saw her mother walk toward her, and her heart melted. She forgot all about her resentment over the too-soon remarriage. She wanted to run into her arms but was restrained by Agatha's hand on her shoulder.

Vance conducted her mother to her, and Roxanne embraced her with a rushing return of the love she'd always felt.

"Did you get my note?" she whispered.

"No, did you write me?" Roxanne asked.

"This morning. We must talk."

Something was not right about the way Vance led her mother to a seat near the orchestra. Sharing confidences that close to the musicians would be an impossibility. Roxanne could not help seeing her mother as a prisoner. Why would that be? Vance had told Roxanne to call, so why prevent their meeting? At least Ian Stone was nowhere to be seen. She was pretty sure his nose was broken. Good for him.

Tanner asked to speak to her before the first set of dances, and she gladly agreed.

"No Stone?" he said.

"With that nose and probably two black eyes? He won't go out in public for a week. Where did you learn to fight like that?"

"Eton. In some ways it's a better training ground than the army."

"Is that where you got that scar?"

"Never mind how I got that. I thought your brother was to appear."

"So did we. He's probably mislaid the letter or forgotten the day."

"He seems very careless of you. Have you ever had to defend yourself before?"

When he reached for her hand, she gave it. "Only against a cut-purse in Exeter."

She could tell Tanner tried not to smile.

"How did you dispatch him? With gunfire?"

"I threw a cabbage at his head. It was a better use for it than trying to sell it."

"And he gave your money back?"

"I took it. He was unconscious."

Tanner choked on a laugh. "I perceive your upbringing may have been as rough and ready as mine."

"Only the last three years. Father's death changed everything."

"How?" He could not help feeling drawn into her life.

"We were suddenly poor. Still are. If not for Aunt Agatha, there would be no ball. I know I should have a thicker skin by now. What do you suppose they are saying, those girls who are tittering their heads off as they line up across from their partners?"

"Pay no attention. They are gossiping about your mother, not us. And I think she knows it. Someone said something that unsettled her."

"Such wicked tongues. How can people bear to be so evil, to discomfort an innocent woman."

"I found out how my mother knew your aunt. They were rivals for the hand of your uncle. Mother lost and married a merchant."

"Perhaps she married him for love," Roxanne said wistfully as they moved toward the other dancers.

"He was not a loving man. Any notions of love or tenderness have come to Holly and me from her."

"What a hard thing. But you are loved by your mother, your sister, and now me—I mean, I shall always stand your friend."

The dance began and they were parted. When they came back together, the startled look had left his gaze. Perhaps he hadn't noted what she let slip.

"The attentions of Captain Harding?"

"I enjoy sparring with him. He is a man of quick wit."

"But I see the way he looks at you. Do you return his affection?"

"No, though I admire him."

"It's June already. If you plan to marry this season, you have so little time. Of course Captain Harding would not be the one to restore your fortunes."

"How mercenary you must think me. If my affections were engaged, fortune or the lack of it would have no bearing on whether I married."

They parted again, and when they came together he looked puzzled once more.

"Of course this discussion is entirely academic," she said.

Tanner frowned at her. "What do you mean?"

"Stone informs me the only suitor his cousin will approve is Ian Stone."

"You will never marry him."

"Of course not. I would rather scrub floors. So I actually have three years to make up my mind."

"Let me lead you in to supper again?"

"So you are not angry about me causing the brawl at Vauxhall?"

"Not with you. I am angry that any man thought he could get away with forcing himself on you."

"But there may be repercussions for you and Holly."

"People have been cutting me all day. Someone must have said something about the fight. They are not giving *me* the cold shoulder because of your mother."

"No, and I was the only one who knew the other participant. Stone must have wanted to make sure no one else offered for me and blabbed about it. Wait till I get my hands on him."

Tanner grinned. "I'll provide the cabbage."

She found herself laughing and thinking the evening could not be so very bad after all. She had told Tanner things she would never reveal to anyone else, not even her brother. That must mean she wanted him for a friend and felt safe with him. She could not have any ulterior motives where he was concerned.

He loved to see her like this, having a good time in spite of all the dangers, real or imagined, in her life. Tanner noticed no one danced with either Roxanne or Holly except Captain Harding, Sir John, and himself, which gave them much time to converse. So those gentlemen asked no one else to dance either but gathered near Agatha, his mother, and her mother. The other ladies had gone to sit beside her even though speech was impossible. Vance remained at his wife's side and danced with no one.

"Is that your brother?" Tanner asked. "Has he emerged from his workshop after all?"

"Fredrick. At last!"

Tanner watched Roxanne run a few steps to greet her

brother, then reduce her pace to a more feminine stride. Yes, she attracted attention—because she was the only true and natural girl in the room besides Holly. But he thought any gossip was motivated by envy, not any real fault in her.

When she began to drag her brother in his direction, he went to meet them. Roxanne and Fredrick resembled each other with their brown curly hair and open features. But Fredrick was no frail scholar. His breadth of shoulder and muscular calves spoke of a man used to working a forge and riding hard.

"Fredrick Whitcomb." He extended his hand toward Tanner.

"I'm Spencer Tanner." He took Whitcomb's outstretched hand.

"So sorry for my tardiness. A spot of trouble on the road. Rox has written of your kindness to her."

"Rox?"

"He would let that slip. Father always said I had rocks in my head."

"We know that's not so. It's her kindness to my sister Holly that drew us into each other's company."

"May I speak to you a moment?" Fredrick asked.

"Oh, you two get acquainted. I shall find Holly so you can meet her."

"What trouble on the road?" Tanner asked.

"A truly incredible adventure. The stagecoach was held up on Houndslow Heath. Fortunately I had a pistol by me and shot the highwayman."

Tanner stared at Fredrick in fascination. "Did he escape?"

"No, so it took some time to figure out what to do with the body. The magistrate was very understanding and let me come on to town, but I will have to give evidence later."

Tanner nodded as though this was all quite normal. He reminded himself not to underestimate Roxanne's brother either.

"Has Rox done anything capricious since coming to town? Aunt Agatha seemed in her letter to hint at so many concerns. But hint only."

This seemed an extraordinary question after he had just confessed to killing a highwayman before he had even reached town.

Tanner replied, "I know of no indiscretion, certainly. There was an incident at Vauxhall where she was importuned by an undesirable, but I happened upon them, so no one could have spoken of that unless he did."

"I'm surprised Rox didn't just bloody his nose herself."

Tanner chuckled. "Knowing her better, I believe she could have dispatched the fellow, but I think she was trying to be on her best behavior."

"That's a relief. So Aunt's fears are groundless."

"Not entirely. You mother and her husband are here."

"Good Lord. Why on earth would they come? That can only bring back all the gossip about Father's ruin and suicide."

"Suicide?" Tanner felt as though he had been hit between the eyes.

"Yes, he was a gambler, often lucky, but as the war ended he lost everything, speculating in the funds, and shot himself. I thought you knew."

"I'm so sorry." A fission of pain shot through his body on behalf of Rox. His comment at the play came back to him. The remark must have stabbed at her like a knife to the heart. If only he had known.

"It was a long time ago. Well, not that long ago. Then Mother married Vance a year to the day after Father's death, adding to the gossip. I suppose I had better say something to Mother, and without the benefit of alcohol in my system."

Tanner swayed on his feet a little when he thought about how Rox had kept her composure in the face of his unknowing attack. Harding must have known, because he took her away to regain her poise. She had not cried or shown her feelings except for the sudden pallor.

Her unique quality was no longer a mystery: not just the courage to face down a bully grappling for a kiss, but the courage to face the whole of London with the tragedy of her father's death on the lips of everyone's tongues.

Looking for a husband was now made impossible by Vance and the reminder of her mother's betrayal. But when Tanner looked at her mother, he did not see a weak woman. She looked like Roxanne, in evident discomfort but not owning to it. Something was not right about the whole situation.

When Tanner led Roxanne in to supper, they arrived at the head table before the others. Roxanne hoped he had forgotten she'd said she loved him. Or perhaps she didn't want him to forget. It had popped out, and she realized the truth of it. She had never trusted men much or counted on them except for Father and Fredrick, but she had a feeling Tanner would stand by her no matter what evil forces tried to destroy her.

That's how she saw Vance and Stone, the embodiment of evil. Her mother, though tired and worried, seemed as strong as ever. But she had a desperate look that Roxanne did not like. Something was seriously wrong.

Once she had settled her skirts, Tanner turned to her and took her hand, his calluses brushing her skin. "I said something the other night at the theater that offended you—indeed, it made you ill. Was it the remark about gambling?"

"You were talking about risk and how it could be courageous, like you trying some new machine, or Captain Harding setting sail in a storm, compared to dicing your fortune away."

"Yes, that is what discomposed you."

"Your ears must be as innocent of town gossip as Holly's. My father diced away his ready, or so I have been told by Captain Vance. And then sold out of the funds when the panic struck. Both those acts seemed wildly out of character for him. Then he shot himself. That was not like him at all, always so resilient and full of life. Sometimes I still can't believe it."

"So your brother said, though he omitted any talk of dice."

"I should say Father enjoyed whist more than dice. That's how he won the *Silverloo*, his yacht. We had such good times on her."

"Are they sure it was not some accident?"

"He was too careful with firearms to have mishandled one even if he had been drinking. I wish I could feel resentment for him, but all I feel is grief. I can handle being poor because of him, but to bear the stigma of blame for his death when it was the last thing I would have thought he would do… He was always so happy. No matter what fortunes befell us, he always said, 'We've got our horses and each other.' I never asked him for anything. He had no need to kill himself for me or Fredrick, either, and certainly not for Mother."

"I'm sure no one thinks any of you are to blame."

"I blame myself. If I had known how desperate he was, I would have talked him out of it."

"I didn't know all of this before. My ignorance of London gets me in trouble all the time. But it never before led me to hurt someone."

"It means much to hear you say that. Of course you don't know all the gossip, and I should not have taken offense at your remark. It was a shock because I was trying to forget. I was so happy that night, and your remark took me by surprise."

"Please, forgive me."

"Of course Harding assured me you meant nothing by it."

"That was good of him."

"Upon reflection, I realized he was right. You are not the sort of person to hurt someone. You're more the hero type, leaping to the defense of silly girls."

"You are not silly. So it was very unwise of Vance and your mother to come to your ball."

"It's the surest way to drive off suitors who might want to marry me. They'll consider me as frivolous and ruinous as Mother. Oh, dear, I had hoped not to speak ill of her. But there it is. How can Fredrick and I be so average, with parents like that?"

"Perhaps they forced you to grow up early in your care of each other."

"Perhaps. At least Fredrick came, and did you see? He danced with Holly. He seemed a little distracted. I'm sure he is inventing something important in his head this very minute."

"Yes, I'm sure as well. Still I'm sorry for what I said."

Roxanne smiled sadly. "It was the truth."

"Then I'm sorry it hurt you."

"It's like a raw wound. I stop my hearing and pretend all the whispering and giggles don't hurt, but they do. I never realized how much until all that gossip was magnified by those evil tongues."

"But what do they say?"

"That there may be insanity in the family, with Father a suicide and Fredrick some mad recluse. I am a singularity. I don't appear to be mad, but they watch me for the slightest sign."

"Ignore them. I want to see your brother's inventions, if he brought his plans. And these chits know nothing. They are jealous of your beauty and self-possession."

"You are being kind."

"I am being truthful, but look. Here they come to sup with us. Your brother has asked Holly, and Harding is doing his duty by your aunt. We shall have a merry time."

Roxanne wished Tanner's prediction had been true, but her aunt, compelled by civility to send Vance and Stone an invitation along with her sister-in-law, had also asked them to eat at the head table, to squash any notion of a rift between the children and their mother. This made any further conversation stilted.

When her mother got up to leave the table, Roxanne asked, "May I call on you tomorrow, Mother?"

She could not mistake her mother's hesitation, but Vance said, "Of course. Send a note round when you are coming."

While the ladies went to the retiring room, Tanner

turned to Fredrick. "I can't tell you how helpful your sister has been. I still have businesses to run and cannot shepherd Holly to every event, so it is good that your aunt has chaperoned them both. Still, another pair of eyes."

"So there is some danger in London?"

"Always. Before the ladies rejoin us, we must speak about what Roxanne thinks we are talking of."

"What is that?" Fredrick drained his glass.

"Your high-pressure steam engine."

"Oh, that. I have reached the limit of my resources. I need to make a cast that can only be forged with great heat."

"So that's your other reason for coming to London."

"Do you know of a mill I could hire? I would need at least three workmen, as well."

"My foundry would do, I think."

"Really. I could rent it and—"

"I was thinking of something more long term. Come see me tomorrow with your designs."

"Wonderful," Fredrick said. "We must discuss this at length."

"You have your plans?"

"Not on me, but upstairs. I sneaked in the back way and changed."

"Come tomorrow afternoon. "I know Sir John and Captain Harding are taking the ladies by carriage to Kensington Gardens."

"Harding? He's from Exeter, isn't he?"

"Yes, Roxanne seems to know him well. Can you vouch for him?"

"Not personally, but he is well thought of, at least by all those who don't engage in smuggling. Rox must have met him on a shopping expedition."

"He seems a complete gentleman to me, yet not a good candidate for her hand."

"I'm quite sure Rox will choose her own husband. She may ask my advice, but whether she takes it..." Fredrick shrugged his skepticism.

They walked past the door to the card room on their way back to the ballroom. It was plain that the four gentlemen who were standing around drinking had been imbibing their late supper.

The phrase "No better than she should be" stopped Tanner in his tracks.

"They could be speaking about anyone." Fredrick grabbed his sleeve.

"But I hear she has an income, if you can stomach the scandal."

"Are they talking about Holly?" Tanner asked. "What scandal?"

"She wasn't palatable even before her mother showed up. Now I'd not have her for all the gold in India."

"No, they are speaking of Rox. Tanner, no."

Tanner wrenched his arm out of Fredrick's grasp and marched into the small salon. The gentleman in question saw him coming but had no idea one of Tanner's hands about his throat would carry him backward into a pillar with very little aid from his own faltering feet.

"Tanner," Fredrick pleaded. "You can't do this here."

"I know," Tanner said. To the sputtering fool in grasp, he said—before a shocked audience—"I'm told it's not polite to just smash your face in, so you will meet me for those words at a time and place of your choosing.

Name your friends…if you think you have any."

"Or apologize, Dalrymple?" Fredrick suggested as he tried to pry Tanner's fingers from around the man's throat.

"He's not apologizing, Fredrick. Will you act for me? I shall ask Captain Harding, as well."

Fredrick used both hands to pry off Tanner's hand. "Perhaps he could apologize if he could breathe."

Tanner loosened his grip and waited, though his large hand was still within strangling distance of the man's throat.

"Dalrymple, do you apologize for this misunderstanding?" Fredrick demanded.

The man coughed and squeaked.

"Just nod," Fredrick prompted.

The young man nodded, and Tanner lowered his arm, sending the man out of the room from the sheer force of his glare. The rest of the men present looked nervously at each other, avoiding eye contact with Tanner.

"We are promised for the next set of dances," Fredrick said lightly. "Let's go."

"Must we? I was looking forward to thrashing him, or someone."

Fredrick nearly dragged him from the room. "Tanner, your wit will be the death of you or someone. You are like a cocked pistol with a hair trigger. One never knows what will set you off."

"I wasn't joking. How could you hear such things said in your aunt's house about your sister and not take exception to them?"

"Although it's perfectly all right for you to assault people in my aunt's house, I may not do so. Besides,

Dalrymple is all mouth. None of the rest of that set are worthy of Rox, and I shall tell her to avoid them."

"I see. You bide your time and squash their chances if they should ever ask for her hand."

"I don't have much power, but I know when to use it. You could wield your wealth like a club. I think I admire you more because you don't."

"And use my fists instead?"

Fredrick laughed. "There's a time and place for everything. I take it from that display you have feelings for Rox."

"Yes, but she doesn't—well, I'm not sure how she feels about me."

"It will be interesting to find out, once word of your challenge gets about."

"I bet you she will think it a great joke."

"Let's hope so. I doubt that Aunt Agatha will."

Chapter Six

Half an hour later, Roxanne was contemplating how perfect Holly and Fredrick looked together when they danced. His black evening clothes contrasted just as vividly against Holly's blush pink gown as did Harding's dress uniform. Of course, it was a country dance. Neither she nor Holly would ever be approved to waltz. She now wondered if she had done the wrong thing by throwing Captain Harding at Holly.

But Fredrick was only playing at having a good time, doing his brotherly duty for her friend. Unless he spent most of his waking hours with his plans and tools, he was not happy. What kind of life would that be for Holly? Of course, Harding had a riskier occupation and was gone on missions frequently.

She must stop thinking about this or she would go mad. Holly must make her own decisions and not marry someone forced on her by her brother or even someone pushed in her direction by Roxanne.

"What is it, Rox?"

She jumped at Tanner's voice, then laughed. "Shall I never live that name down?"

"Dance with me, and I will school myself to recall your Christian name."

"We have already danced twice."

"Who makes these rules and who keeps score?" he complained, then glared at a knot of matrons in the corner of the salon. "Well, there is not a rule against talking to unattached girls when no one else wants to dance with them. Come and sit with me." He took her arm and led her to an unoccupied sofa.

Roxanne felt sure there was also a rule against them sitting together when not under the gaze of a relative, but she let it pass. "So did Fredrick tell you about his steam engine? He uses a small one to work the bellows for his forge."

"Yes and that he is trying to cast a heavier pressure vessel, and about his applications for compact steam engines. We need to talk at length. I can help him at my foundry."

"Ah, that is what I wish above all. We drive to Kensington tomorrow. It would be the perfect time for you to meet."

Tanner smiled down at her. "I wonder why I didn't think of that."

Roxanne laughed. "By your look of mock surprise, I see you did think of it and scheduled a meeting already."

"Am I so readable?"

"Not always. I don't know you as well as I know Fredrick, but generally I can figure out what people are thinking, see the wheels turning in their heads, so to speak."

"What about Harding?" Tanner bent his gaze on the captain, who was dancing with any female Lady Sherbourne introduced to him.

"Poor fellow. Aunt Agatha is making shameless use of him to entertain those misses, even though the men of the ton shun us. Harding keeps wishing for another war so he can get a better ship, as if hunting down smugglers and pirates is not dangerous enough."

"So you are sure of your…feelings about him?"

"There is nothing between Harding and me, if those are the words you are fumbling for. I know Aunt expects me to find a husband among the *ton*, but frankly, I think this has all been a huge mistake. There is no one I can talk to among that set."

"Except me? Or am I just a cit to you?"

She turned toward him and laughed. "You'll be happy to know I hold you above them in my esteem. You work and have good sense besides being Holly's brother. Of course you understand me. We are like-minded souls."

"I'm happy you think that's the case, for I have something to confess to you."

"What have you done?" She was prepared to upbraid him, but perceived a glint of humor in his eye.

"Challenged a guest for making disparaging remarks about your income."

"To a duel? But Tanner, you could be killed!" She grasped his sleeve before she realized what she was doing, then let go of him. "You must cry off from it. Whatever he said about my income was probably true and is not worth your life. Promise me you will not go forward with such a challenge."

He patted her hand in a comforting way. "Your brother persuaded Dalrymple to apologize."

"That fool? His is one of the few names I remember among the *ton*, because he is such an idiot." Though she seldom employed her fan, she plied it now since anger overheated her, replacing the chilling fear of Tanner being shot.

"I thought it ill-advised of him to criticize you in

your aunt's house. So you don't mind that I defended you?"

"Of course not, but I should think he would run shy of a fight with you. Only if a mouth was a dangerous weapon could he consider himself well-armed."

Tanner chuckled his agreement. "But that's the unfortunate point. In this nest of vipers, a mouth *is* a dangerous weapon. There are likely to be repercussions."

She found herself unable to repress a giggle. "That does it. Tell me all, or I will wrest the truth from Fredrick."

Tanner complied and reduced her to laughter again.

"So you are not angry with me."

"What would a ball be without a little excitement? Besides, I don't plan to find a husband among these fops."

"What about Sir John? He might draw back."

"Strangely enough, it almost comes as a relief to know that Vance will refuse Sir John if he asks for my hand."

"I didn't think you would accept Sir John anyway."

"I don't feel anything for him except sympathy. He is past his prime and has foolishly let his son take over his affairs."

"He's a knight. Not a grand enough title?"

"Don't tease me. As if I care. But I would hate to be the one to refuse him. His intentions are kind, and he does speak knowledgeably on some matters."

"Horses and hunting."

"Yes, but there is one area in which he falls short."

"What is that?"

"He never argues with me no matter how much I provoke him. And that is a problem."

Tanner grinned. "How dull. Are you willing to wait for your freedom?"

"In three years, I'll be twenty-one. What I don't want is to be a burden to my brother."

"How could you ever be a burden?"

"It's worse being in the way. If he marries, his wife will keep house for him."

"That's not being in the way."

"When you are used to running a place, even a small place, you can't ever hand those reins over. Clearly I must do something with my life. Perhaps I should become a governess."

Tanner coughed. "Spare me that image."

"I know a lot. I think I could be a good governess."

"No mother would hire you; you're far too pretty."

"Is that a compliment, and an unsolicited one as well?"

"It was, and I meant it. You should have a life, be able to travel or do what you want."

"There is an obstacle to all those goals: marriage. I begin to hate the idea."

"So once you get your freedom, you will keep it?"

"I think freedom is an illusion. We spend our whole lives building cages around ourselves with our choices."

"I never thought of it that way."

"Your business is part of your cage. But you enjoy work, so you do not wish to escape it. Mother, Vance, my aunt, and even Fredrick are part of my cage. A husband would be the biggest bar of all."

She noticed her aunt looking in her direction and wondered if this was a signal she was supposed to try to mingle. Then she realized this discussion of marriage and her views was working against her where Tanner was concerned. Why did she always say the wrong thing? Marriage to him could be heaven. But how could she enjoy a lovely future when her mother was stuck with Vance?

"Marriage doesn't have to be a trap. It could be a meeting of minds. You need someone to take care of you."

She looked wistfully toward her mother when he said this, but Vance had not left her side, so any useful conversation would be impossible, especially with the orchestra in their ears. Certainly marriage was a trap for her.

"A good marriage can be a wonderful thing. My parents had such a marriage, but I'd rather take care of myself, or at least be sure that I can. Perhaps I'll just disappear one day."

He caught her hand and raised his fingers over hers in a touch so gentle a bit of wind might have been blowing against her fingers. "Don't run away."

"I was only joking. Remember, I'm trapped, and as cages go, it's not such an unpleasant one." She turned her hand to clasp his, palm to palm, enjoying the rough reality of his calluses against her skin.

"If a man promised you as much freedom as you wished, could you stomach marriage then?"

His gaze seemed so earnest.

"Is there such a paragon among men?"

"A paragon? No, but someone who wishes to be with you forever."

Roxanne realized that however much she enjoyed this jousting she should not lead Tanner on. "Marriage is not the only problem. It's my lack of trust. Do you understand me? The problem is with me, not your white knight."

"I'm speaking of myself, of course."

"I certainly hope so. Can you deal with a person who has so many insecurities?"

"I think I would enjoy vanquishing them one by one."

"There is a problem with knights, you know." Roxanne pulled her hand away.

"What problem?"

"They tilt at everything. I'm not used to having all my foes vanquished for me. My knight would have to leave some of them to my devices."

His lips twitched into a smile. "Tell me which ones."

"My mother's entrapment. I must solve that before I can enjoy any happiness for myself. Do you trust me to do that?" She looked once again in her mother's direction. She should go and try to speak to her even if the violins set her teeth on edge.

"I trust you to tell me if you need my help."

"Then we understand each other."

He slowly shook his head in wonder. "For my part, not even remotely, but I will try to have the patience to wait."

Roxanne smiled at him, though it was a guarded smile, and went to seek her aunt.

Meanwhile, Spencer kept trying to think why he was so attracted to Rox. Yes, he would let himself think of her by this endearment her brother had introduced.

It could be the girl's startling confidences, or her unique beauty. Finally he decided it must be their similarities. Instead of asking him for things or services, she told him she would rather do things for herself. He had never met any woman like her before.

Holly came to look for him, and he realized people had been departing for some time. On the way home in the carriage, he kept going over his conversation with Roxanne. He had declared himself and she had deferred her decision, yet he did not feel rejected. He had never met a woman so vocal in his life or one who thought so deeply about people or cared so much.

He was glad she had told him the truth of her situation, but she had mentioned more than one problem. No, she had called them dangers, at one point, and he had no idea what they all were. Poverty would be vanquished once Fredrick started working with him, and her feeling of responsibility to her brother could be said to be satisfied, though by rights Fredrick was the one who should be taking care of Roxanne.

Her mother might be constrained by embarrassment rather than by Vance himself. Perhaps if she and Roxanne could only speak to each other in some setting where they did not have to shout, that situation could be resolved.

Vance had to be the biggest danger, since he could refuse any offer she received until she reached her majority. When he asked himself if he was willing to wait three years to marry her, the answer was a resounding *yes*. In this day and age, Vance could not force her to marry Ian Stone. And Tanner rather thought he had vanquished that foe anyway.

The carriage had earlier taken his mother home after the light supper, so once it returned for them, he had only Holly to see home.

"You look happy," he said as he handed her one of the lit candles on the hall table.

"I had a wonderful time because I decided to stop

worrying about what people thought of me."

"Rox—Roxanne's advice?"

"How did you guess? I wish I were more like her. Good night, Spencer. Aren't you coming to bed?"

"In a little while. I have some work to do before morning."

"Spencer, it is morning."

"I know." He took his candle into the study and lit a branch of candles, but he did not address the pile of letters on his desk. He handled the firm's correspondence here, where it was easier to think, rather than at the foundry. The wool mill was so remote he did not visit it more than once a month.

He sat at the desk but didn't want to think about work tonight. Tanner thought about his life, what he really wanted. Making money was easy compared to making a life that you enjoyed. He had known Roxanne Whitcomb less than a week and now knew that his life would be incomplete without her. Was this love? He certainly hoped so, even though she seemed less romantic about their relationship than he did.

He wasn't sure how he had expected to approach a prospective bride. Apply to her father, he supposed, and if his money was good enough, then ask the woman without much preamble if she wanted to clap hands and make a bargain of it. He shook his head sadly.

In Roxanne's case, she operated with an illusion of freedom, though she was apparently more constrained than any of them had realized. He hoped Fredrick would be her guardian once he came of age, for he really could not see himself treating with Captain Vance for her hand. He'd much rather smash the man's face in for thrusting Ian Stone on her.

He got up and went to gaze out the window into the quiet square. After all his education, why was violence more than guile his best first option? He was patient when it came to work, to business. But in real life he demanded action of himself, which is why he was ill-equipped for society gossip and games. He was so fortunate that Rox had no patience either. They were meant for each other.

He had to wonder if part of her allure was that she had turned him down. She needed him a great deal less than he needed her. He wanted so desperately to do something to make himself worthy of her trust, but when what she wanted was the freedom to solve her own problems, playing the knight or any kind of hero was difficult. All he could do was be ready for her to call on him if she ever thought to do so.

Apparently she had spent the last three years taking care of herself and her abstracted brother. Straightened circumstances had honed her purpose to a thin edge. She wanted her brother to find investors and succeed with his inventions. But what for herself? Did she want nothing beyond reconciling with her mother?

And that was a strange situation, that Rox couldn't get to speak to her. Why would her mother return if she did not want to reunite with her children? All questions and no answers.

As open as she was, Tanner suspected there was something Roxanne was holding back, some danger too vague to define, or some impediment she did not think he could help her overcome.

He recalled the look of her holding the bench leg like a cudgel, even in her filmy evening dress, and chuckled to himself. At first he had been shocked at her willingness to throw herself into the fray. But then he admired the way she took the emergency in stride.

Whether he attained her hand or not, courting Roxanne Whitcomb would prove to be the biggest adventure of his life. He would have to plan some entertainments where her unconventional behavior shone—or at least where there were fewer of the *ton* to witness it.

It came to him that Harding might make a better match for her than himself. His occupation held the element of danger and would require a wife to manage on her own for extended times. Yet, much as he liked Harding, he would not give up the field to him. Roxanne might prove too much for the young officer to handle.

Chapter Seven

Kensington Gardens was beautiful and amusing. It should have been peaceful, since they had chosen a sunny day for the drive. Surely her aunt and Holly's mother seemed to be enjoying the walks when they left the carriage to get a better look at the flower beds. Sir John patiently took each of them on an arm, while she and Holly walked beside Captain Harding.

Roxanne had sent a note to her own mother about the expedition, but received no reply. She began to suspect that her mother did not get any of her notes. By their short exchange last night, she inferred she may not have gotten her letters, either. What to do about Vance was a problem that could ruin the day if she worried over it. Nothing could be done about him for the moment.

Without Tanner, the expedition lost its spice anyway. She realized she enjoyed jousting with him even more than matching wits with Captain Harding, and she really couldn't argue with Harding in Holly's presence. Harding always called yield, but Tanner never did. She kept telling herself she was the one who had conspired to leave Fredrick and him home, yet somehow she wished Tanner could have come as well.

"What say you to that idea, Roxanne?"

"What idea? I wasn't attending."

Harding laughed. "Sir John has proposed letting us ride his hacks in the park."

"I should love to ride in London."

"I don't know how to ride," Holly said.

"Sir John can teach you, can't you, sir?" Roxanne asked, though she knew full well she was competent to teach Holly to ride. It seemed a kindness to defer to him, since they were his horses.

The older man smiled benignly on Holly. "I'd be delighted."

"We had better discuss this with Spencer first," her mother replied. "Horses are so dangerous."

"I would like to ride tomorrow," Roxanne said. "Who knows how long the sunny weather will last. What about you, Harding?"

"I can ride and I do enjoy it, but tomorrow I must see to the final rigging of my ship."

"Aunt, may I go, at least?" Roxanne begged.

"Now, dear, it would better if you were one of a party."

"We shall have a groom with us. That will be unexceptionable," Sir John stated.

"Oh, very well," Lady Sherbourne agreed.

"I just hope my riding habit still fits." Roxanne thought about how difficult it was to converse while riding, so this would be the perfect way to spend time with Sir John without having to talk to him.

****

Tanner hated putting off his meeting with Fredrick, but this interview, however unpleasant, could not wait. The son of an earl was coming to ask for Holly's hand and though Kemerly was only a viscount now, he was his father's heir. This was exactly the sort of match Tanner's father had envisioned for Holly. He just wished his mother wasn't wandering about Kensington Gardens, tiring herself, when he so badly needed her advice.

And he sincerely hoped Kemerly was not one of the men in the card room from the night before. Surely none of them would ever approach him for his sister's hand. He tried to call to mind their faces and failed. Never mind his chances of remembering their names. The fact that anyone was applying for Holly's hand meant either that no gossip derived from his threats to Dalrymple, that Kemerly and his father were immured to such gossip, or that Holly's settlements would cancel out her brother's rude manners.

He pushed the papers around on his desk, but none of them had anything to do with Kemerly or his family. He never went into a business deal blind, yet he was planning to do just that, and with his sister's future as the stakes. A week ago, he might not have felt these tremors of doubt, but Rox had shaken his views on the *ton*. They were not all good people. Kemerly might be in debt or might be a gamester like Roxanne's father. And since Tanner was outside the gossip net of the *ton*, he had no way of knowing anything.

If his mother were here, she could recite the man's lineage and tell him the worst about the whole family. Moreover, she could tell him what the man looked like and if he had ever met him before. Damn his faulty memory. The name meant nothing to him.

How would Fredrick handle such an interview? He would know whether the man was an acceptable candidate or not. The *ton* was a closed circle, and Spencer began to question the wisdom of trying to invade it.

****

When Roxanne got home to luncheon, she was

expecting to hear Fredrick babbling about how much Tanner had loved his inventions. She was miffed when she discovered that nothing had gone forward about Fredrick's plans. Tanner had called off the meeting with some excuse about an interview he had to conduct. And Fredrick had not even inquired what it was that took precedence over his engine.

She felt resentful, as though a task she had crossed off her list as completed was still hanging over her head. It completely destroyed her appetite, and she scarcely touched the food on her plate.

Fredrick, on the other hand, devoured the soup and salmon with gusto. "Tomorrow will be time enough," he assured her. "We are to meet tomorrow morning. Tanner does not attend church either. It will keep Aunt Agatha from ringing a peal over my head for not escorting you. Why are you in such fidgets? We don't even know if Tanner will be interested in my work."

"Because I want it settled. I want your future secure."

"Why. What's the hurry?" Fredrick turned his attention to his cutlets.

"Also, there is no answer from Mother. Vance said I could see her today, and she has not replied to my note. Does it strike you that she seems more like his prisoner than his wife?"

Her Aunt Agatha stared at her as though she had run mad, then glanced consciously at the servants. "Whatever gave you that notion, dear? I'm sure it is no such thing."

"Mother seems so constrained now, as though she is afraid to speak in front of Vance. Fredrick, do you think she is being held against her will?"

"No. The idea never entered my head. Send another note inviting her to ride to church with you. Make sure the footman delivers it into her hand."

"Yes, if only that would work." She pushed her plate aside to go to the morning room and pen the letter, trying to make it sound as though she was not worried.

Then she went to her chamber and searched for her riding dress, which must be crushed into a wrinkled mess in her trunk somewhere, and she still wondered if, once found, it would fit at all. Why was she so upset that Tanner's meeting with Fredrick had been put off a day?

She stopped as she was sliding her trunk across the floor. Was it because that would mean she didn't have to marry for money? Moreover, she could show her avid interest in Tanner without seeming like a scheming witch who was trying to get preferment for her brother?

But could she suddenly embark on a wild flirtation with Tanner when she had been at such pains to treat him in a brotherly way? Would she not still seem scheming, even if he and Fredrick made a deal about the inventions?

Tanner had as much as declared himself the night before, and that was without even seeing Fredrick's plans. Was that not enough demonstration of his regard, that he wanted her in spite of her insecurities? What obstacles lay in the path to her happiness?

She realized there were three. She plopped down on the bed to enumerate them as she dug through the clothes she had brought from Exeter. She did not feel she could abandon her brother until she knew he was on the road to prosperity. She acted as though he could not take care of himself when actually he was a most able person. She should strike him off the list of obstacles—but somehow could not.

The second was her mother, who seemed a virtual prisoner of Lucius Vance. How could she be happy when her mother so clearly was not?

The third was herself, her sense of obligation to others that kept her from considering herself. If she agreed to marry Tanner before her brother was settled and her mother rescued, she would feel like the most selfish person alive. Logic argued against this stand, but feelings could not be denied.

She did what she always did when her head felt about to explode—she made a list of her goals. First of all, she had to figure out if her mother was a prisoner and, if so, contrive a way to free her from a husband she could not want. Secondly, she had to figure out how to get herself out of Vance's clutches. Fredrick would be free of him within a few days, when he turned twenty-one, but depending on how her father's will had been written, she might still be under Vance's thumb.

It did occur to her that Vance's death would solve both these difficulties, but she didn't think herself capable of murder, even when sorely provoked. And having been a soldier, Vance probably wasn't going to meet with a convenient accident. She could ask Tanner to kill him, but that hardly seemed fair to Tanner. He had no quarrel with Vance.

Her third problem was getting Fredrick set up so she could deal with her feelings for Tanner. If Tanner did not want to support his inventions, would she be willing to try to persuade him to do so after marriage? She thought not.

Sir John was a difficulty, as well, since she liked him and did not want to hurt him. Clearly the solution to that was to refuse him immediately. But he would think she had been leading him on. How had this gotten so complicated?

There was her buff summer riding dress and jacket, at the very bottom of the trunk. Or…not the very bottom, for under it was the box with her father's dueling pistol. She could not explain even to herself why she had brought that reminder of the tragedy. Perhaps her grief was so much a part of her she would never leave it behind.

If Roxanne married anyone but Tanner, she would miss Holly desperately. She'd never had a sister and did not want to lose that friendship. Of course, Holly would no doubt marry soon, and that was an additional worry.

Who would Tanner choose for Holly? She could not trust his judgment where members of the *ton* were concerned. If he was not blind to his sister's preferences, Tanner would by now realize Holly and Harding were in love. But if she pointed that out to Tanner, he might forbid Harding the house.

She stood and pulled the skirt on over her muslin dress, then managed to fasten it. One problem solved, a small one. When her maid came in, Roxanne requested she try to press the dress for tomorrow.

She paused and sat on the bed when she realized what would take precedence, for Tanner, over steam engines and pressure vessels. He was talking to a suitor. So she had to add to her problems that her very best friend might suddenly be married to the worst possible man because Tanner didn't know what he was about. She had been playing up the best qualities of being a man of business over a gentleman of leisure, but Tanner didn't seem to take that to heart.

Roxanne needed a plan of action. She would make a

surprise call on the town house and see if she could get at her mother. She needed to find out the terms of the will. If her mother did not know, then she had to call on her father's man of business and get him to disclose them. She must keep a low profile with both Tanner and Sir John until Fredrick was of age and she knew where she stood. Why had she jumped at the chance to ride with Sir John tomorrow morning?

She had accepted Sir John's offer because she did miss her old life, with the horses and the carefree rides. But she had responsibilities now, and one of those was to talk Tanner out of marrying Holly to someone disgusting. How to interfere in that decision without appearing to was yet another problem.

Distressing to think that her very own white knight was one of her problems. She had better try to vanquish some of the others before she tackled him.

Chapter Eight

Roxanne was subdued as she waited for Sir John to appear. Earlier she had stopped at the town house to see if her mother wished to drive to church with them, but she had been turned away by a servant. The footman who'd delivered her note yesterday had not been able to get past the kitchen door.

What was going on? She racked her brain to recall what trick she could use to get into the house that used to be her home, and she came up with one or two notions that might work, but not today. She would be able to slip away from her aunt tomorrow when her seamstress was making a call at the house.

She expected a ride with Sir John to be just as boring as a drive, but the chance to get on horseback again after three years tempted her to an outing when she had almost decided to never see Sir John again.

He and a groom came with the horses, and she was glad he sat his hack well. Much could be forgiven a man who could ride. The mare the groom led seemed familiar to her and nickered when she stroked its nose. Then she realized it was her very own mare, which had been sold on her father's death. She'd thought never to see Mist again, and here the gray was looking still eager for a run.

She took the reins and led the mare to the mounting block herself, then sprang onto her back much in her old style.

"That was agile of you."

"I know this mare, sir. I owned her for the first half of her life."

"Indeed. I had no idea. My son suggested her as a trusty mount for a lady."

"She is that, and most eager to please. Shall we go?"

As they rode sedately up Oxford Street toward the park, Rox realized that Mist brought back bad memories as well as good, most of all a realization of everything she had lost. So her eyes were full of tears when they reached the corner entrance and started along the northern bridle path where they could trot.

"Are you all right?"

"These are tears of happiness, I assure you."

"She could be yours again if you marry me."

"Only if I marry you? You mean you would not sell her to me?" It was a moot point. She could never afford to buy Mist back except by trading herself for the horse. Was she willing to pay that price?

"It would seem she is my only advantage in the contest for your hand."

"I have never understood why anyone would want to marry me."

"But my dear, you are charming. There's no one else quite like you."

"Now you have me worried. In what way am I a singularity?"

"You are so disarmingly frank."

"Oh." She felt the frown forming on her brow. That was bad, wasn't it?

"You say exactly what you mean. You don't flirt and simper."

"Frank, am I? Then I ask you plainly, is marriage the

only way to get my mare back?"

"Yes."

"What about a wager?"

"What have you to wager?"

"My hand in marriage. You have said yourself that I am a woman of my word. We are almost to the pond. If I beat you to the Serpentine, I get my horse back. If you win the race, I agree to marry you."

"And get your horse back." He laughed at her startled look.

"Yes, I suppose that isn't quite fair, since I win in either case, but the odds are against me. You have that great black brute and are riding astride. I'm on this tiny mare and riding sidesaddle."

"But you might fall. You could be killed."

"Mist knows me. She won't throw me."

"But your reputation! If you win, you are ruined. Look at all the people strolling the gardens."

"If I win, I won't care. If I lose, you will marry me and my reputation does not matter. Or does it matter to you perhaps too much?"

"I own to a wish to wed you before you do anything outrageous, for I really do like you and feel you would be the perfect woman with which to start a second family."

That took her aback, for it was the first time he had mentioned children. "Is your first family wearing on you?"

"My son is my estate manager, and he and his wife are always underfoot. There is also the concern that she might be barren. No children in all these years."

"I had not realized that."

"I am the head of my house and wish my name to

continue. Only men worry about such things."

"I see. Your line must go on by whatever means."

"My second concern is that you would make a bet."

"Yes, the stigma of my father's fate. I never thought of him as a gambler." She was near the beginnings of anger now. Of course it was stupid to race in Hyde Park where anyone could see her, but she suddenly didn't care what anyone thought of her. She only cared about no more rides on Mist as they were meant to be, gliding across a green field with their hearts keeping time to the hoofbeats.

"Is there no other way I can win you?" he asked.

Roxanne tightened her hands on the reins. "I think not."

"Very well, I accept your challenge."

She turned Mist and halted her, pointing toward the manmade lake. "I play fair. You say when to start."

"Go."

What she had counted on and Sir John had not was her setting out cross-country rather than taking the paths he intended. Of course any horse would be faster on turf than on gravel. Not to mention how Mist could drop into a smooth gallop at the slightest urging. The ground rolled away under them like a dream, with her almost flat along the mare's neck. Her euphoria lasted until she saw a commanding figure on a chestnut take a start at the vision of her and Mist flowing along the ground. The chestnut's hoofbeats were added to those of the mare, Sir John's hack, and the groom's.

She pulled up at the lake and was walking Mist by the time Sir John got to the Serpentine. Tanner had more ground to cover, so she was hoping his storm would not burst over her head until Sir John had conceded. Perhaps all the park saunterers who had noted them would think it was a runaway.

"By God, you win—what a starter she is! If I'd known, I would not have raced her. I suppose this means you are shut of me."

"No, I like you quite well, and you may continue to call. It's just that I'm not sure I'm cut out for marriage at all."

"I hope you change your mind about that."

Tanner rode up with a face almost as red as his horse. "What are you doing?"

"Winning. Something I've had small experience of, lately."

"But no lady gallops in the park."

"It's my fault, Tanner," Sir John claimed. "I accepted the bet."

"Bet?" Tanner glared at Roxanne.

"If she won the race she won the horse and I unfortunately did not win her. But I continue to admire her no matter what anyone else says."

"That is a good thing, for she may get no other offers than yours, after this display."

"Then perhaps I have a chance after all. Shall I escort you home, Miss—"

"I shall see her home," Tanner almost shouted.

"Until tonight, then," Sir John said and touched the brim of his hat in salute.

"Until dinner tonight," Roxanne replied.

Tanner watched Sir John join his groom and ride off, then started to walk his horse. Roxanne eased her hold on the reins, and the mare came up beside them. Mist was a little hot but looked as though she would like another gallop.

"You are angry," she said.

"Yes."

"About the gallop or about the bet?"

"Both."

"I'm glad I did it. There's not a soul in London who understands me or cares about me except Fredrick and Holly." She paused to see if he would add his name to the very short list, but he kept his mouth clamped shut. "If I have put myself beyond the reach of everyone, that's a good thing."

"What about your aunt, or your mother?"

"They are mine to face, not yours." She glanced at him, but all he showed was his stern profile. It was as well that she'd found out early how much the approval of society really meant to him. He was not the man she thought he was.

"I must ask that you do not see Holly again." His voice sounded cold and impersonal.

"Afraid my courage may rub off on her?"

"Your lack of judgment."

"Holly has plenty of sense, enough to realize all the men she meets want only her fortune. And you set her up for failure. If she turns them all down, she disappoints you. If she accepts one, she makes herself a prisoner for life. Think about that, Tanner, since you are having such stirrings of conscience on my behalf."

"Marrying her to someone with a title is something we've talked about for years."

Roxanne snorted. "Something you want, not Holly and probably not even your mother. You talk about your only sister as though she is an object to get out of the way so you can get back to work, and you have not even the grace to feel bad about it the way Fredrick does."

"Why have you saved all this condemnation till now? Do you see that I am no longer a possible target for you?"

"Target? That is cutting. You never were in my sites, if that's how you want to think of it."

"Then what was the attraction? For you did seem to enjoy our company."

"A true friend, something I have never had." She felt his gaze on her. "Nor I think Holly, either. I had hoped you would relent, give her another season to find her own way, but the only man she cares about is ineligible, as far as you are concerned. For a cit, you set too high a price."

"What man?" he demanded. "Fredrick?"

"Tanner, are you blind? You don't even know?"

"Tell me," Tanner ordered.

"No, you learn for yourself. Wake up and pay attention. Holly will need you, if you have forbidden me to see her again. If you think I have been using you, then think how you were using me, Sir John, and Harding to keep her safe."

When they got to her aunt's house, Roxanne told the groom Mist was a gift from Sir John. She knew that servant's gossip meant a great deal more than any story the *ton* invented. If word got out that Sir John had given her the horse, then the speculation would be that she would marry him. And perhaps she should. She could do far worse for herself. He was old but a perfect gentleman, with a sense of justice and a surprising amount of wit, now that she knew him better. Besides, he needed to be rescued from his son and daughter-in-law.

She watched as Tanner cantered out into the street. She must have angered him, indeed. But all that she said to him had to be said by someone, and she knew Holly would not have the courage or Harding the effrontery. She went inside to explain to Aunt Agatha her new acquisition and brace her for the storm to come.

Her aunt took the news better than she had hoped. When asked if the dinner was to be canceled, she said certainly not, so Roxanne went upstairs to pack away her riding costume. But she stopped herself. Mist was hers and she would never let anyone take her away again. It was Vance who had said the horses must all be sold to settle their debts. But her father had always had a reputation for being beforehand with the world. What debts?

It was while she was sitting at the window going over in her mind the ride and why she had done it that a strange thought occurred to her. What if her father had not killed himself? What if all their misfortunes were a fiction Lucius Vance had invented? He had said he was her father's best friend. But her father had never mentioned Vance before, let alone as a close friend.

That brought her to the unwelcome conclusion that Vance had murdered her father and taken over the estate for his own profit. But how had be worked it? Fredrick had been at school and barely got home in time for the funeral. He had accepted Vance's tale and seemed eager to get back to Oxford. It wasn't that he had not cared, but he was not good at personal relationships or consoling people.

She'd been sent to a finishing school until Fredrick had graduated. That did not speak of a lack of funds. Only after Vance and her mother had married did she learn that Vance was leasing the main house. He had somehow convinced them it was an act of charity, that they were impoverished and he was helping.

When she remembered her father, she could not reconcile him committing suicide and leaving them in such straights. He was a courageous man and would have faced any difficulties with them.

What her suppositions led to was a more terrifying conclusion than her father's murder. Vance meant to kill her brother so he would not inherit. That's why he needed his cousin's help, if Stone even was his cousin.

She had thought there were only a few obligations standing between her and Tanner, but there were many. Of course, a real knight would slay some of these dragons for her. But the conclusions she had reached sounded fantastic even in her own mind. The levelheaded Tanner would not believe her, and that was a disquieting thought. Still, she should give him the chance to aid in her rescue.

That was, if she had not offended him to the point of him cutting the connection. There was also the worry that Vance's evil might spread to encompass the Tanners if they involved themselves with her. Assuming Fredrick would not believe a warning from her, she was on her own.

Chapter Nine

Tanner had ridden out onto the heath to vent his anger but then realized all he was doing was tiring his horse. He apologized to the beast and took him back to town at an easy walk. He had been attracted to Rox, had actually proposed to her only to be turned down. At least he'd been spared the embarrassment of applying to her brother. How could he have been so mistaken in her character?

Or was she as practiced at deceit as she was at flirtation? Surely she'd known she could best Sir John in a race or she wouldn't have bet. So if she had bet on a sure thing, was she indeed the gambler he feared her to be? His mind was still churning with images of Rox, snippets of delightful conversation, mixed with the bald truth she had just delivered like a punch in the gut. She might have lied to him about her reasons for not wanting to marry him, but she had told the truth about Holly. The man who had asked for her hand was eligible in every way, but when Tanner informed Holly of the fellow's intentions, she'd burst into tears.

When he finally got home, he came in from the stable to the drawing room, still in a turmoil over Rox, and discovered his sister in the arms of Fredrick Whitcomb.

"What the devil is going on?" Tanner demanded.

Holly turned on him with a vengeance, her face

tearstained and her handkerchief sodden. "It's you and your wicked temper, Spencer. You have berated Roxanne, and now I shall never see her again."

Fredrick actually looked relieved when Holly left his arms and stomped toward Spencer.

"You are behaving very unlike yourself, Holly."

"What do you know about what I'm really like? Who cares if Roxanne galloped in the park?"

"I never thought to warn her," Fredrick said. "That should have been my job, if only I'd come up to town with her."

Tanner tossed his hat on the table. "Common sense should have reined her in."

"And Sir John gave her the horse," Holly said.

"She won it from him in a bet." Tanner watched Holly's face for some sign of outrage, but she still glared at him as though this was all his fault.

"There was a groom?" Fredrick asked.

"Yes. After I caught up with them, I escorted her to your aunt's. Sir John went his own way with the groom. Rox told the stable lad the mare was a gift, which means the *ton* will expect a proposal from Sir John and her acceptance."

Fredrick dipped his head in agreement. "And what did Sir John say?"

"That he will see her tonight at your aunt's dinner."

"I suppose it could be worse," Fredrick said. "If we all go on as we have been, we may brush through this."

Holly wiped her eyes and glared at him. "She was my only friend, and now it's all ruined. She won't go anywhere with me, and I'll be all alone again."

Tanner blew out a tired breath. "Don't be so dramatic, Holly. You're never alone."

"You don't know what it's like. You have work. Mother and I will have no visitors." Her tears began streaming again, and Tanner felt that two outbursts from her in one day were more than he could face.

Then he wondered if him making her cry earlier in the day had sent him on his ride in a foul mood. That would be why he had ripped up at Rox so badly.

"I'm sure you're exaggerating. Someone will call."

"You're blind, Spencer. You don't really care about anything but appearances. And then you nearly engaged me to a man I loathe."

Her anger was a slight improvement over her tears. Fortunately, he had made no agreement with Kemerly, not even a verbal understanding, since he had still wanted to consult with his mother. "I told you I would not force you into the match."

Harding was shown in, and though his color was high, he smiled tightly and came toward Holly with a note. He delivered it with a curt bow and nearly clicked his heels together.

"Is this from Roxanne?" she asked.

"Yes, she wanted to let you know the dinner is still on, but if Tanner forbids your coming, she will understand."

"If Mother is going, Spencer can hardly forbid my attendance. I hope Roxanne is not much upset by Tanner's high-handed treatment of her."

"Miss Whitcomb is more durable than most. The question is, how did she put it? Do you have the courage to be seen with her?"

"Of course I do." When Holly dried her eyes and left the room, Tanner found himself staring after her in surprise.

Harding bent his gaze on Tanner. "I don't know what you've said to Miss Whitcomb, but I'd keep my distance from her, if I were you. She's detailed several ways she may kill you and has already consigned your soul to the devil."

Harding left Tanner blinking in shock. For a second, he'd almost thought Harding meant to call him out, but the threat had been from Rox. How like her.

Fredrick laughed. "That sounds more like Rox. Sorry, but your face! You're not angry?"

"Not at her anymore. What business was it of mine to censure her behavior? I agree with her judgment of me."

"You must be the only man in the world who would rather have a woman damning your eyes than see her crying."

"I can't imagine Rox crying or in despair."

"As to that, I'm sure she hides it well. I have given her enough cause. Well, this is no day for business, I think."

"No, I want to discuss your designs."

Fredrick reached for a leather case. "I brought them with me."

"I meant your designs on my sister."

"Ah, I have no such designs. I'm as surprised as you that she would seek comfort in the arms of a total stranger rather than confide in her brother. But I never have understood women."

"Apparently neither have I."

"I should be going."

"No, bring your drawings into the library. I have to get my mind off women or I'll go mad."

Tanner felt vacant when he led Fredrick into the

normally restful book-lined room, but as the drawings rolled out in front of him he was able to lay aside the scene with Rox and how he could have handled it differently.

"So you can see that the stronger the steam vessel the more power, and if we alternate the piston bursts we don't lose as much energy."

"And this is all in aid of pumping water?"

"Oh, Lord, no, though that is what I started doing, mine drainage. The merchants need a faster way of getting fleeces to market in the southwest. They used to raise all they need, but now fleeces must come from all over. Then the wool, if not used where it is cleaned and spun, must go to factories for dying and weaving. I want to make a compact steam engine that will move wagons of fleeces."

"On the roads."

"If they were in better repair. But currently there are small sections of rails in various areas. They used to be wooden, but more and more are cast in iron. Now rail wagons are pulled by teams of horses. If we replace those with small engines capable of moving those carts, all we need is a supply of coal."

"And those same carts can carry coal."

"Yes and more coal than fleeces, because it's less bulky. The bounds are limitless."

Tanner looked at Fredrick. "You're speaking of a steam railway."

"On a small scale, and using rights of way already established. You must have track-moving carts in your factory."

"Yes, drawn by teams."

"Ten horses could be put back into agriculture with

one such engine, which does not need to rest. And the fleeces can be shifted to steam carts with carriage wheels to run on the roads where there are no tracks. Unfortunately, I don't bring anything to this table but my plans and offer of hard work," Fredrick finished up rather breathlessly.

Tanner nodded and smiled. "Will you work for me initially? The ownership remains yours, but we must proceed with this. It's too important not to."

"Gladly. When may I see your smelting factory?"

"Now."

"But it's Sunday."

"The only day it is quiet. Let's go."

As Tanner showed Fredrick around the smelting area, the chain-making shop, and the shed with the great molds where they forged anchors, half his mind was still on Rox, how beautiful she had looked when he condemned her for galloping in the park. He had never seen such a flush to her cheeks. No other young lady of his acquaintance would own to having a fit of temper, and she had actually warned him that arguing was one of her avocations.

When you thought about the gallop like that, it seemed a small thing. She had raced a horse in the park and would be regarded as fast by everyone in the *ton*. What business was that of his? He tried to tell himself it was because Rox's reputation might reflect on Holly, but he had more than enough applicants for Holly's hand. They had been reluctant to show much interest in her in public, but the notes kept arriving. That might mean each of them planned to wall her up at a country estate and simply take advantage of her income.

If he admitted the truth, his anger was because of

how Rox would reflect on him if she had accepted his proposal. Perhaps it was his fault. He had proposed to her, but when she seemed hesitant, he had given her the space she said she needed. If only he had pushed her to accept him before the ride with Sir John, none of this would have happened. She would have accepted his offer and there would have been no ride, no bet, no race. Was this ride with Sir John a way of discouraging Tanner's interest? It had not put Sir John off, but it had stopped Tanner in his tracks.

He thought of her bright eyes and defiant smile. She had looked more alive today than at any time since he'd met her, and that was saying much. He could not convince himself that she would have accepted his proposal, or that even if she had she would have foregone the race, would have restrained her emotions. She was not the wife for him. Or perhaps it was simply that he was not the husband for her.

By the time they finished their inspection and preliminary plans, it was time to drive home and change for dinner. If he was still received by Lady Sherbourne, he would have to contrive a moment when he could apologize to Rox for his presumption and try to figure out if there were any tatters of their friendship left.

Tanner was received and greeted by Lady Sherbourne as though nothing had happened. Rox cast Tanner a cold indifferent look as Holly went to sit beside her on the window seat. His mother began a close dialogue with Lady Sherbourne. That left Tanner with no choice but to make conversation with Harding until Fredrick came down from changing.

Rox stood up when Sir John was shown into the drawing room.

"Sir John, so good of you to come," Agatha said.

"It was the least I could do, since I was the agent of Miss Whitcomb's disgrace."

"Keep nothing from us," Agatha said. "We are all friends here."

Rox nodded. "Only tell me it is complete and that I may shake the dust of London from my hem."

"Not by any means, at least not among the gentlemen. They admire you immensely."

Roxanne tilted her head, trying to make sense of this upshot. "And none of the ladies liked me before anyway. How ironic."

Sir John came to take her hands in his. "Hold your head high and smile. You did well to tell your groom the horse was a gift. Of course, now, an offer is expected from me, and I should make one even if you choose to refuse it, but we have time enough for that later."

"So I may sponsor Roxanne to those entertainments for which we already hold cards?" Agatha asked.

"To fail to appear would be social suicide."

Tanner watched Rox's face go pale and freeze. Sir John had no idea what that one word did to her. Surely he knew the circumstances of her father's death. How then could he mention suicide so carelessly? The man was insensitive in the extreme.

"Holly may accompany you," Tanner said. "That is, if you agree, Mother."

"Yes, of course."

"May as well all sink together," Tanner said, then downed his sherry.

Both Fredrick and Harding chuckled.

"But it's not funny," Agatha said. "Whatever made you do it, child?"

"I'm not sure. Suddenly with the mare under me, ready for a run, it was three years ago and the world was as bright and sunny for a few moments as it had ever been. And then I remembered why I am where I am today."

Holly reached her hands to hold one of Rox's and smiled at her.

"Thank you all for standing by me." She squeezed Holly's small hands. "You have taught me what friendship is. Now let us forget today and enjoy good company no matter what tomorrow brings."

She glanced up uncertainly at Tanner near the end of this speech, but looked away too quickly to read any expression in his eyes. He was not sure what message he wished to convey.

They were a normal party for a time, talking and laughing as they dined, Rox perhaps more so than the others, but she was faking it. He could tell. When it was time for the ladies to move back to the drawing room to allow the men to enjoy their port, he excused himself and caught up with her in the hall.

"What do you plan to do now?" he asked.

She turned and looked vacantly at him. "About what?"

"Your marriage, your reputation."

She shook her head. "Believe me, Tanner, those are the least of my worries."

"What else could concern you?"

"I had best not tell you, for I have a feeling you would never believe me."

"You just reaffirmed our friendship. What is there that you cannot share with me?"

She seemed to be in the midst of some internal

struggle, and he tried to let his sympathy show in his eyes. Finally she licked her lips, which had gone a bit pale.

"I suspect Vance of murdering my father and rewriting his will."

Tanner choked on the apology he had been memorizing. "What start is this?"

"I have not been permitted to speak to Mother, and I believe she is his prisoner."

"She must have married him of her own free will."

She gazed at him with troubled eyes. "I doubt that."

"Then why?" Tanner felt as though the floor was tipping under his feet.

"I don't know, but I will find out if I can get her alone. Also I must call on our solicitor to see if I can get any information out of him."

"By yourself?"

Rox hesitated. "I suppose I must. Fredrick does not take me seriously."

"Take my advice and forget this fantastic plot you have imagined."

"But Tanner, I told you my father was not the sort of person to kill himself."

"No one is until driven into the last ditch."

"Only a coward would do such a thing, and he was no coward." A flush of anger crept into her cheeks.

"But if your father gambled it all away…"

"I don't think he did. I think that's a lie Vance made up to explain stealing all our money."

"Rox, you've become unhinged." He reached for her hand, but she pulled away.

"Don't help me, then. See if I care. Just watch out for Fredrick."

Tanner staggered back and bumped into a table. "What has Fredrick to fear?"

"Vance, of course. If Fredrick dies before his birthday, Lucius Vance will get everything."

"There isn't anything to get."

"He may have lied about that as well."

She turned to leave him, but he grabbed her arm.

"This is a flight of fantasy. You are setting yourself up for disappointment."

She stared at his hand until her let her go. "No, I'm just seeing clearly for the first time in three years. It's the only possible explanation. If that is all you have to say, that I am unhinged, I will see you later. I knew how you would be, what you would say. Why did I confide in you?"

There were a thousand things he wanted to say to her. He wanted to protect and care for her. He wanted to marry her before it was too late. He was sorry for his angry treatment of her. But before he could decide where to start, she turned on her heel and left him, apology and protestations of love undelivered like a stillborn baby.

Chapter Ten

The next day, Spencer sat brooding in his office at the foundry when his manager came in to get the materials list Fredrick had left with them. "What do you think, Randall? Will it work?"

"It's brilliant, sir. I can have two workmen build a mold in a few days' time."

"No, not yet. I want the inventor to be in charge of that."

"Not your idea, then?"

"No. I'll let you know when I am ready."

"But you could have had this same idea yourself. We go ahead and build the thing while he is still looking for backing, and it's yours."

Tanner stared at the drawings, not wanting to make eye contact with the man while rage boiled within him. He had known this foreman since he was a lad, but this was the first time the man had said anything that left him stunned. "Are you suggesting I steal this design?"

"It's the way of the world, sir." Randal shrugged and made for the door with the list.

Tanner's rage boiled over when he realized Randall had quoted his father. "Not my world." He got up and snatched the list from Randall. "You are dismissed."

"What?"

"Discharged."

"But I worked for your father for thirty years."

"And you shall have your pension, but I won't consort with a thief."

"Just how do you think your father acquired all his wealth? By the sweat of his brow? Not likely. He stole and swindled his way into this foundry and that beautiful house."

"If that's the case, it will require looking into." Tanner waited until Randall had cleared out, then went down to the floor to recover the drawings and appoint the foundry foreman as temporary manager.

He tried to get back to work but could only review in his own mind the considerable evidence that his father was less upright than he had hoped. Finally, he went home with all of Fredrick's plans safely in his possession, hoping he had not put them at peril. He must see his man of business tomorrow to see what part of Fredrick's designs could be patented for the boy immediately.

There were so many men working on steam engines that they must move fast to try to get a patent on Fredrick's high-pressure design before someone else did.

"How did it go today?" his mother asked from her seat at her escritoire in the green-and-gold morning room. He noticed she was writing checks. Probably her quarterly contributions to her benevolent societies. It was unusual for him to seek her out in the middle of the afternoon, so well she might ask. Tanner seated himself in a chair he drew up to the desk.

"I won't bore you with the details, but his designs are innovative, and I plan to bring him into the business."

"So you've forgiven Roxanne?"

"I had no right to condemn her. Indeed, I owe her an apology and missed my chance last night. But she is having trouble facing reality."

"You think she should marry Sir John?"

"No, he's too old for her. She'd run the show, and she's too young for so much responsibility."

"So were you when you took over the business. I hope you did not tell her so."

"She did not ask my opinion. I have never been good at admitting when I am wrong, but I see now the need for it."

"Good. Apologize to Roxanne." She patted his hand and turned back to her desk, apparently considering the interview over.

He got up and walked to the window that looked down on a small rose garden. After his father died, Tanner had the garden made for his mother, to remind her of the country. "I need to talk to you about something else. The business."

"Your judgment has never erred."

"I fired Randall today because he suggested I steal Whitcomb's designs."

"Oh, Spencer! You would never have considered such a thing."

He turned and saw her hand arrested in the air, the ink drying on her pen.

"No, but would Father have done it, as Randall claimed?"

She looked at him a long moment and tossed the pen back in the holder. "Yes, which is why Randall thought he was on safe ground to suggest it." She shook sand on the bit of paper in front of her, then tapped it clean.

"So our fortune is made on the backs of workingmen."

"And women. You smile at me for my charitable

works, but it is the only way to salve my conscience about our fortune."

"I should do something about it."

She rose with a sigh and came to stand beside him. "There is plenty you have done already. You pay the workers a living wage, you've improved conditions in the foundry and the wool mill. You see that their children are educated, and you pension them when they are sick or old rather than simply letting them go."

"You seem to know a great deal about what I do. Why have you not spoken sooner?"

"Because you seemed to be finding your own way to the correct path. You are not your father, no matter what anyone says."

"And the anyone is Holly. I am sorry for that. Advise me now on how I can put things right with her."

"Start by letting Holly have her head. Why does she have to marry this year? She's only seventeen. She doesn't like any of the men of the *ton* and feels more comfortable in the company of Roxanne and Captain Harding."

Spencer nodded his agreement. "He has his uses."

"I know you are using him to entertain the girls when you cannot guard them, but when you say it like that, it seems so…"

"Mercenary?" Tanner sat on the windowsill, wishing he had broached the subject of his father a long time ago.

"Somewhat."

"I have come to the conclusion that Father was not an honorable man."

"He didn't break the law, as far as I know, but he didn't tell me much about the business."

"I can see why."

"He never confided in me, and I was glad for it. He was a hard man, an uncompromising man. It frightens me that I see a little of him in you sometimes."

"How so?"

She laid a hand on his shoulder. "You're climbing a ladder, the one society has dictated, and you're dragging Holly and me with you without asking if that's where we want to go."

"Who wouldn't want to be accepted by the *ton*, invited everywhere?"

"Me. I like to see my friends, though I have few of those left. But the social whirl bores me. And I suspect Holly doesn't like it much either."

"But that's the point of all this work, this wealth—to give you a better life."

"Is this better? And you continue to pursue wealth when we have enough, more than enough. Why?"

"Because it's so easy," he said. "Once you have capital, making more money is a matter of giving orders."

"But what is the real cost?" She let her hand drop. "You look confused."

"I treat everyone fairly."

"Everyone who works for you. But what about the people who support your industry…the boys who sort the coal, the miners who die in flooded mines." She ended with her hands clenched together in front of her as though she had prepared this speech and had been only waiting to give it.

"I can't control all of that."

"But you can do something. You can buy a mine and run it well. Show the world what can be done if you care."

"All that takes time. Fredrick and I are working on a project that will help even more. No more being kicked by horses when a steam engine can move fleeces and coal and a thousand other things."

"I understand that, and I understand your ambition. I don't admire your personal goal."

"I want to make your life better."

"And I want you to make *everyone's* life better, in so far as possible."

"So this conversation *is* about your charitable works? I said you could spend your whole allowance on the poor and I will give you more."

"I do and you do, but I can only help educate and feed them. You can actually change their lives." She stoked his cheek and made him want to do as she wished.

"But what do you want for yourself?"

"To see you and Holly married to people you love, not ones who will raise your social status. I want you both to be happy."

"I'm happy."

"You think you are, but even you must see that your sister is not."

"Short of a fortune hunter, she may marry anyone who pleases you."

His mother tilted her head and smiled. "Good. I shall hold you to that promise."

"Does she actually have someone in mind?"

"How like you not to be able to see. That's all, Spencer. I will give Holly the good news."

He left the room thinking he had never been so summarily dismissed in his life. It was as though his mother had called for him and now, the lesson over, she was sending him away. He wondered how she had been patient with him so long.

****

"Are you sure this is the right place?" Holly asked.

Roxanne craned her neck to look up at the sign that hung over the sidewalk on Grey's Inn Road and almost strained it when Holly grabbed her hand and pulled her out of the path of a team and wagon. They pushed the door open, ringing a noisy bell over the entry.

"This is the business of Fenster and Son, Solicitors. We'll just go up and see. You may wait in the carriage if you wish, Holly."

"Abandon you now?" Holly looked shocked. "Certainly not."

When they reached the landing, a dour clerk in a rumpled suit scowled at them over a ledger. "Wot do you want?" he asked emitting a strong scent of garlic and onions from his lunch.

"I want to see Mister Fenster, my father's solicitor."

"The elder or the younger?"

"It must have been the elder."

"He's dead."

"Then I'll see the younger."

"No you won't. He's in court."

"When will he be back?"

"'Ow should I know?"

Roxanne blew out an impatient breath. "May I make an appointment for tomorrow?"

"He takes appointments on Wednesdays."

"The day after tomorrow. Very well, what time?"

"Between one and two."

"I shall come back at one on Wednesday then."

"There'll be a line," the clerk warned.

"Put my name down. Miss Roxanne Whitcomb."

She thought the name made the clerk curl his eyebrows as though her reputation had preceded her. But that was probably just her imagination. What could this law clerk know about her, after all?

"Well, he was less than helpful," Holly said as they were handed back into the carriage by the footman. She brushed some dust off the hem of her dress.

"I think we need reinforcements," Roxanne said as the carriage moved forward.

"Would Fredrick come?"

"No, I mentioned it to him, and he shrugged it off. He's too busy with his work."

"What about Spencer?"

"Even worse. He thinks I'm deranged."

"That leaves Captain Harding and Sir John."

"I don't want to involve Sir John, and Harding's so busy."

"Let me ask him. After all, he will be sailing back to Exeter soon, and we won't see him again."

"You sound as forlorn as Harding. Can you believe Tanner doesn't realize Harding is in love with you?"

"Tanner has no clue or he wouldn't let him run free in the house. I'm sure he thinks Harding hasn't the gumption to ask for my hand."

"And does he?"

"Oh, I hope so."

****

Tanner was still brooding in his study when his butler announced Captain Lucius Vance with an impassive face. Tanner didn't read faces all that well, but for Thorton, impassive translated to disapproving.

After a moment's thought, Tanner decided to make

Vance come to him rather than join him in the drawing room. "Show him in here."

Was that because he felt more in control in his study, or because he did not think Vance rated the drawing room? For the moment, he could not say. He did rise to shake his hand and indicate a chair on the other side of his impressive desk.

"I hope I do not interrupt your work." Vance glanced at the stacks of letters at Tanner's elbows.

Tanner took a moment to decide if that was a gibe or not. Probably, but he did work and would not be embarrassed by that. "Correspondence can always wait. May I offer you some brandy or sherry?"

"Thank you, but I can stay only a moment." Vance sighed and crossed his legs.

"And your errand?" Tanner prompted.

"Well you may wonder, for I hesitate to carry gossip even when there does seem to be a pressing need to inform you of certain matters."

"And I hesitate to listen to gossip at any time, so are we at an impasse already?"

"Reluctantly I must overcome my distaste and warn you of some danger to your sister's reputation."

Tanner sat up straight in his chair. "Indeed. What is the nature of the danger?"

"She is often in the company of my ward, Roxanne Whitcomb."

"I am well aware of it." He was also aware of how much Rox hated Vance.

"And by your tone, I take it you don't approve."

"Of course I approve the friendship. Miss Whitcomb has done nothing to gain my censure." Tanner expected a diatribe on the park incident.

"The gossip about her father hangs over her like a dark cloud."

Tanner stared at Vance, whose eyes did not meet his except for an occasional glance. Vance was assessing the effect of everything he said to Tanner.

"A cloud called to mind by your return to London at the worst possible time."

"I agree. I counseled her mother to wait, to deny herself the pleasure of seeing Roxanne make her come out because it might cost her dear, but she would not listen. My regard for my wife is such that I bowed to her desires even though I did not agree." Vance opened his hands as though he had been helpless in the matter.

"So it was her idea to come?"

"I had to make an appearance to deal with the legal matter of handing over the remnants of Fredrick's estate to him, but I would have kept out of the public eye for that. Now I hear the sad tale of her father's suicide on every corner."

"Perhaps a slight exaggeration. But what has all this to do with Holly?"

"Roxanne turned down the only sure suitor for her hand that I could think of, my cousin, Ian Stone. In fact she incited an incident between Stone and you at Vauxhall Gardens."

"I incited the incident. Miss Whitcomb had nothing to do with it."

"Be that as it may, I expected her to have to wait for marriage until the gossip died down again. I even speculated taking her back to Paris with us, hoping some foreign connection would not mind or not have heard—"

"I understand what you mean. I'm still waiting to hear how Holly comes into it."

"Merely by association with Roxanne and the man she is about to make a misalliance with."

"Captain Harding? I assure you Miss Whitcomb has no interest in Harding. Besides, they were acquainted before she came to London. If there were anything between them, he would have acted on it before."

"I may have seen this Captain Harding you speak of, but I know nothing against him. It is Sir John Marbrey that I fear she will marry."

"Fear? But he is well-respected, a paragon among the *ton*. I have never heard a word against him. So if you have some sordid—"

Vance waved his fingers languidly. "Nothing like that. Sir John's misfortunes, alas, are not of his own making. His son is a gamester, and you can well guess where that has led. The daughter-in-law has so far managed to hide the damage her husband's proclivities have caused. Sir John is done up, and all that has been mortgaged will be lost. He'll be left only with his entailed country house and nothing to maintain it."

Tanner rose and strode to the window, seeking the right questions to ask. "How can you suddenly come into this knowledge when you have been abroad for two years?"

"When it became clear that my ward had a preference for Sir John, I made inquiries and was shocked at what I found out."

Tanner swung around and stared at him. "Then tell her this yourself."

Another big sigh. "There's the problem. Miss Whitcomb, in her grief over her father and her lost fortune, has decided to blame me for every evil that has befallen her. I don't care what she says of me. I have no stake in the *ton* and prefer to live abroad anyway. Once my obligations to my dead friend are fulfilled, Miss Whitcomb may marry as she chooses, for good or ill, but I do not wish her to attempt such a misalliance on my watch, so to speak."

"She cannot marry without your permission, so don't give it."

Vance nodded. "She cannot legally marry without it, and that puts me on the horns of a dilemma. Do I give it and have her marry a pauper, or withhold it and risk a scandalous elopement?"

Tanner folded his arms and stared, hoping to get Vance to make eye contact at least once. "So you want me to tell her."

"Would you? Coming from me, the news would either be thrown back in my face or she would run headlong into marriage just to thwart me."

"What makes you think she would marry Sir John if she knew?"

Vance looked thoughtful for a moment, as though composing a speech. "You have some brief acquaintance with my ward. You know she is self-sacrificing. If she has a flaw, it is that she is too noble. If she thought Sir John was ruined, she might just decide to marry him anyway and share her small portion with him."

Tanner had to admit in his own mind that this reading of Rox's character was accurate. "What does it matter if the news comes from you or me, if you think she will try to rescue him anyway?" He leaned on the window ledge and waited.

"I think she would not hate you for delivering such news. She might actually listen to your good counsel, whereas she would never heed mine."

Tanner recognized the truth of that statement, but he had the strange feeling the truth was being subverted and used against him in this case. "You ask me to play a villain to both Miss Whitcomb and Sir John."

"I ask you to save her from her better nature. And there is the matter of your sister's reputation. The news of Sir John's ruin will seep out over the next few weeks, and my ward will once again be the focus of gossip among the *ton*. Every place your sister goes with her, she will also share this unfortunate notoriety. If you won't do this to save Roxanne, do it for your sister." Vance ran a hand over his brow as though he was out of argument.

"I will consider what you have said." Tanner stood up to signal the interview was over but knew better than to promise Vance anything.

"That is all I ask." Vance too rose from his chair. "I know I said I could stay only a minute, but I realize I have taken much of your time. Be aware that I regard you in esteem. Your foundry and others like it were instrumental in the victory in the recent war. Even though I did not take part in the last battle, I value those who made our success possible. If you were to consider marriage to my ward, I would be receptive to your request. I simply do not wish to see her make a misalliance and be in want again."

Vance turned and walked toward the door. Tanner stared at him but could find no flaw in his speech, though it went counter to what he would have expected from Vance. Had the man just offered Rox up as a sacrifice to get his way in this?

"I will remember what you have said, and I will speak to Miss Whitcomb. I trust that you will hold this interview and what you know of Sir John's situation in confidence."

Vance turned with his hand on the doorknob. "You have my word on it, but the tradesmen and the servants know, so the rest of the world will not be far behind them. Please act today."

Tanner walked toward him. "Sir John is an honorable man. Once he knows, he will not contemplate marriage."

Vance's brow wrinkled with worry. "But if they are betrothed when he finds out, will Miss Whitcomb follow her heart or her head? I think you know the answer to that." Vance shook his head again and left.

Tanner blew out a long sigh. He felt as though he'd been asked to be the firing squad for an innocent man. He passed all of the interview back though his head and could not see anything that Vance was doing wrong. And yet he had the feeling of being used.

Of course he was being used to deliver the blow that Vance did not want to, but was it for good or ill? He could only talk to Rox and let her decide what to do. The biggest surprise was Vance's ready consent to the notion of a match between him and Roxanne. That felt like a trap in some way he had not figured out yet. Was it a lie? Would Vance later withhold his permission, once Sir John was no longer a contender, or did Vance see some advantage to having Rox married to a very wealthy man?

Tanner found himself reluctant to think of Vance even as a distant relation. If Tanner and Rox married and Vance ran aground, wouldn't he be compelled to rescue him for the sake of Rox's mother? In the end, Tanner wasn't so disturbed about how much Vance knew regarding Sir John's affairs but how much he had clearly studied Tanner's business.

He found himself wishing for counsel, and there was none. If Rox had overheard this interview, she would put the proper spin on things. So the only way to figure out what she thought was to deliver this unwelcome news to her. But he decided he would have to withhold the bit about Vance being willing to sacrifice Rox to him. That would only hurt her.

As soon as Roxanne returned Holly home from their morning of shopping, Tanner rode his chestnut hack toward Manchester Square and left it with a groom in the stable. Early in the day he'd sent a note round asking if Rox would like to ride and found a reply on his return with an emphatic yes.

He let the knocker fall, hoping he could be more vocal on horseback than in the drawing room, or that Rox would have forgotten her bizarre fears of yesterday. He now had two things to say to Rox that he would rather not be distracted from. He was shown into the drawing room where both ladies were present.

"This is the first time you have called since the dinner," Agatha chided.

"I've been busy with Fredrick's designs. He's amazingly talented."

"So have I been busy," Rox said. "But a ride in such weather is not to be missed. Who knows when the rains will keep us indoors after this."

Agatha rose and said something about having tea ready for them when they returned. Rox led the way downstairs and to the back door where her mare now stood, saddled and waiting as well. His chestnut touched noses with Mist and pawed the ground in his eagerness to be off.

Suddenly Rox blushed, and Tanner realized she

might have the notion he was going to propose again. He had done nothing as a preamble to that suspicion. What sort of idiot would attempt it on horseback anyway? She had no reason to think after their last encounter that he thought better of her, yet he could see that her hope stirred. Perhaps he should have offered to take her driving instead. He helped her mount, and she let him.

As they walked the horses sedately out into the street, he said, "First of all, I want to apologize for my interference in your—for my criticism of your riding."

"You were sorely provoked, and one of the more charming things about you is that you are not cool but do lose your temper when annoyed."

"Charming? Now *you* are flattering *me*."

"You make me feel less guilty about losing my temper. So that was the first of all. Is there a second item on your agenda?"

"It pains me to admit this, and I have seldom had to say such a thing to anyone before, but you were right."

She looked puzzled now rather than flustered, and she was trying to smile at his backhanded compliment.

"I was? About what?"

"Sir John. It would be unwise to accept a proposal from him."

Roxanne looked confused. "But he has not proposed."

"He hinted that he would." He watched her glance back and forth between him and her mare, a strain for her, since he sat somewhat higher in the saddle. Then he realized he was blocking her view of the street and he should stop distracting her until they made it safely across.

Once they passed through the park gate and set the

horses on the bridle path, she said, "But he hasn't. Why are you warning me away from him?"

"It's all a show. He owes more than he can ever pay, and his affairs are in the hands of his son and daughter-in-law."

"But why then would they not discourage him from pursuing a penniless debutante? Moreover, why would he give me an expensive mare?"

"I don't know. At least you found out in time."

"That may be just gossip. We should not jump to conclusions."

"The way you did yesterday with much less evidence?" Oh, no, why had he brought that up?

She glanced up at him, then loosened her reins and gave the mare the signal to trot. "You just apologized for interfering in my life, and you seem to be at it again."

He felt himself grimacing. "Ironic, isn't it?"

"The ironic part is that I begged you to help me find out about my own affairs and you refused. Yet you meddle in Sir John's finances, perhaps engendering some unfavorable gossip for him by doing so."

"I did not meddle. I was told this in confidence."

He could see a frown mar her brow.

"By whom?" Rox demanded.

"By your guardian, Vance, who requested I drop a word in your ear. He did not think you would listen to him."

"A poisoned word." Her agitation communicated itself to the mare, and if not for Rox's firm hand on the reins, the horse would have bolted into a gallop again.

"And you said what?" she asked.

"That he should tell you himself."

"Very well, you are acquitted of meddling, but I

would not have believed him. Why did you?" She spun away from him onto a cross path, and for a moment he thought she was going to let the restless mare have her head, but Rox kept her to a steady trot.

"Why would he lie?"

"Knowing Vance only slightly, I can't imagine, but he does have a reason for everything. This is absurd. Sir John has unlimited resources, properties all over. He cannot be done up as you say."

"Your father squandered his whole fortune without you being any the wiser. Is it out of the realm of possibility that Sir John's son and daughter-in-law have beggared him without his knowing it?"

"But unlike me, Sir John can get an audience with his solicitor and find out what's going on. You would know if you were ruined."

"But I'm an accountant."

She stared at him, and he wondered what she was thinking.

"He actually called at your house? Why did he divulge this to you and no one else?"

"He appeared this morning before I went to the city. Vance told me for Holly's sake, as well."

"Sir John has not been paying addresses to her."

"You know that, but you are frequently all in company. Vance thought it prudent to warn both of you."

"Through you," she mused.

"It's my job to protect her from fortune hunters."

Rox shook her head. "Which is why you are dangling her in front of them. She needs another year or she will do something desperate just to get out from under your overbearing ways."

"I am not overbearing," he shouted.

She turned her head and leveled a condemning gaze at him from under the brim of her forage cap. "Examine your conscience. I think you will find that I am right at least about that."

Roxanne had more to say to Tanner, but he kept a bit ahead of her horse. She would have had to shout to make herself heard over the creak of the leather saddles and the jingling of the bridles. If he wished to pout, so be it. She was not going to let him destroy her pleasure in this fine day.

Perhaps he would not ask her to ride again. That was a bleak thought, but she could go with a groom, and certainly Sir John might take her again. She was half dreading to see Sir John today. Though she had an answer for him, she almost hoped he would not ask the question.

Tanner maintained his silence until they returned home, and since he knew how much she liked to argue, she thought he had done it just to punish her.

"I have done my duty," he said as he helped her down from her mare. "Now you have to decide what you are going to do."

"You have not given me enough information to make a decision."

"I have warned you." He mounted his horse again and left her in the stable yard.

Roxanne saw the curtain in the morning room window move and looked up to see her aunt watching her. She went upstairs to discover tea had been laid.

"What did you say to Mr. Tanner?" Aunt Agatha asked.

"The truth."

"Oh, well, that explains it. I'm sure he's no longer a

possibility."

"I'm not sure he ever was."

"No new invitations in the post today. I really think that if Sir John offers for you, you should accept him." Her aunt looked up at her to assess her reaction to this suggestion.

Roxanne took the cup her aunt handed her. The older woman seemed to be hanging on her unspoken words. At least Sir John was kind and honorable. He didn't always listen to her either, but he didn't argue with her. "Yes, I shall make no impediment."

"Really, you agree with me?"

"That's not unprecedented."

"It is lately."

What had she just decided? Sir John did not argue with her, but wasn't that one of the things she liked best about Tanner, that he argued?

Her throat almost closed, so she took another sip of tea. "Is Fredrick home?"

"Mr. Fredrick just drove into the stable yard," Greeves said.

"I must see him."

"Sit and finish your tea first."

Roxanne had small hope of convincing Fredrick to confront the solicitor, at least not before his birthday, but she had to try. It wasn't just his fortune and future at stake. It could be his neck, as well.

Fredrick did not listen to her either. He cared about her but he always thought he was right and shrugged off her fears.

Why had she decided to fall in love with Tanner, who would be just as difficult a cross to bear as Fredrick? Perhaps love wasn't a choice. It had seemed to sneak up on her and plant itself in her heart deeper with every meeting with Tanner. Rooting out her love for him would be difficult, but she must if she meant to retain her identity.

It was imperative someone take action to save her mother and Fredrick. How could Tanner be so impulsive in small matters, like beating up Stone or strangling Dalrymple, and not take action when her family was at stake?

Tanner demanded proof. She was not going to let the proof be her brother's dead body. Someone had to listen to her. If not, she would protect them herself.

Chapter Eleven

Roxanne stared at a coddled egg with disfavor the next morning. Though the bread was toasted perfectly and the tea well made, she could not enjoy the smell or sight of food. Without a visit from Tanner to anticipate, the day started out dull. Then she heard a carriage pull up to the front steps.

It was unprecedented for a gentleman to call before noon, yet Sir John was waiting for them when they left the breakfast parlor. She took it from the damp on his coat that it was raining. And she had been so abstracted she had not even noticed.

"May I have a word with Mr. Whitcomb?"

"You've missed him," Agatha said. "He went out already."

"Then Miss Whitcomb?"

"Certainly, Sir John. You may speak to her in the morning room."

Roxanne preceded him into the room, wondering which tack she should take in replying to his proposal.

"You know why I am here."

She turned to face him. "Yes, I do."

"Will you accept me as your husband?"

"I admire and like you, sir." She could see his face fall and followed his gaze to her hands, which she had clenched tightly in front of her.

"But you do not love me."

"How you put words in my mouth. I do not love anyone that way. Perhaps I am not of a romantic nature."

"Then you will consider my proposal?" He came toward her and took one of her hands, forcing her to stop squeezing them together.

She hesitated, then swallowed her pride. "Unfortunately, I am not free to follow my will in this. My guardian, Lucius Vance, informs me that he alone can make that decision for me."

"I had thought your brother would be the man to apply to."

"When Fredrick comes into his majority in a few days, I think he should be able to speak for me, but I do not know the terms of my father's will."

"Then I must apply to Vance?"

"I counsel you to wait." She reached out to him and laid her free hand on the damp sleeve of his coat. "Vance has a wicked tongue and has been spreading rumors about the soundness of your finances."

He turned an astounded gaze upon her.

"I apologize for conveying this gossip to you, but I feel you should know."

"Then I may have to call him out after I ask for your hand."

"I beg you not to do that. He is a hardened soldier and might kill you just for spite."

"You forget I used to be a soldier as well." He patted her hand, but Roxanne felt far from reassured.

Sir John left with a look of determination that almost seemed romantic. Roxanne began to feel like a character in a novel, and she did not like it. Characters often simply had things happen to them and tried to make the best of bad situations. She had much rather take some action to prevent disaster.

But what? It wasn't fair that women were so powerless. Even if they had money they could not do what they liked with it. Her own maid had more freedom than Roxanne did.

Aunt Agatha crept into the room. "Did he offer for you?"

"Yes." She closed her eyes, trying to blot out Sir John's determined gaze.

"Did you accept?"

"Yes."

"Now we're getting somewhere."

"I asked him to wait a few days before making any announcement, since Vance is still my guardian."

"That seems prudent. You outrun my expectations."

Her aunt came and hugged her, making Roxanne feel even more powerless. She should never have come to London. She'd enjoyed life more in Exeter, where she at least did useful work keeping house and growing vegetables. Probably the hired boy had not weeded the cabbages or beans, and they would have nothing for fall.

"What's the matter, dear? I know he is only a knight, and the daughter of a baron should have been able to look higher."

"Baronet. Father was a baronet."

"Don't quibble. Considering the mischance of your mother's appearance, I think we are lucky to get Sir John for you."

Roxanne hated that she had played the Vance card on sweet Sir John, and she also felt as though she had just sent a man to execution. Perhaps Tanner could intervene between Sir John and Vance, but would he even listen to her after she had just chided him over interfering in her affairs? Could she dare to ask for his aid after what he had said to her? Rather, after what she had said to him. And why did they argue at almost every meeting?

He didn't take her seriously, her fears and worries, so he made her feel belittled even though she was doing everything she could to solve her problems. She would like to be willing to rely on some strong hero. And she would love that hero to be Tanner instead of Sir John, but she had turned down Tanner's offer to slay all her dragons. Since Fredrick was unresponsive, it looked as though she was going to have to make do with herself. She should at least apologize for her latest rant at Tanner. The mess of her life was not of his doing and should not be his concern.

He usually came in with Fredrick on the way back from the foundry. It was often late, since they were working on the engine casting after the daily work was complete. Perhaps she could have a word with him then. To think she had hoped he was going to propose to her again yesterday. Or had he been thinking of it and had she ruined it? Clearly she was not a suitable wife, if she drove him away, yet she couldn't be that mercenary person she had expected of herself. She had discovered she could not marry for money, and now she realized she couldn't marry just to gain protection. If she married Sir John, she would be the one defending him against interfering family.

She wrote another note to her mother and sent it round, but she no longer expected a reply from her. She hated doing nothing. She would much rather take action than wait, especially when she had nothing to wait for. She went over her problems in her head but saw no solution to any of them. If she even had a plan, that would be something. But other than trying to sneak in to see her mother, there was nothing she could do. And Fredrick's birthday was day after tomorrow.

****

This was what Tanner loved, making his way home through the dark streets after a day's work well done. It was a long walk across the bridge from Southwark clear to Mayfair, but he could so seldom find a hackney in the neighborhood of his foundry at night. It made no sense to keep a team standing about when he never knew how long he would be.

The rain had washed the air and made the city smell crisp if not clean. When they got to his house, if Whitcomb decided to stop in, they could raid the kitchen and wine cellar.

He was focusing too much on cold beef, cheese, and a Bordeaux when something smashed into his shoulder. Fredrick went down beside him, similarly accosted. Tanner grappled with his attacker, kicked him in the knee, and wrested the cudgel away from him.

A stream of foreign invective startled him, but he spun and flogged one of Fredrick's assailants as hard as he could with the club, knocking the man senseless. Fredrick was almost unconscious but still gamely punching away at the other thief.

Tanner dropped the block of wood for fear of hitting Fredrick and wrenched the footpad off his friend. Several punches to the gut took the man out of the fight. The first man was struggling to his feet, but one move from Tanner sent him hopping away. How cowardly to flee and save his own skin.

Fredrick struggled to his feet, heaving and blowing,

but collapsed against Tanner. Clearly getting him medical help took precedence over finding the watch to arrest the footpads. Tanner threw Fredrick's arm over his shoulder and grasped his belt with his other hand, pretty much carrying his whole weight up St. James Street in the hope of finding a hackney.

There he hailed one who was trolling for theatergoers, but the driver demanded Tanner pay in advance, having assumed they were drunks. Of all the nights for such a thing to happen. If her brother was disabled, Roxanne would never forgive him.

Roxanne stood staring out the window into the darkening street. "They are at the foundry very late."

Her aunt looked up from the book she was reading. "Perhaps we should send the carriage for them. The streets are dangerous."

That her aunt was worried did not bode well. "My brother might not like to know I don't trust him to take care of himself, but I don't."

"Yes, imagine his stagecoach being held up on Houndslow Heath. What is the world coming to?"

"What?"

"He made light of that incident, but he could have died," her aunt confided. "The day of your ball, too. It made him terribly late. He didn't want to worry you. Oh, bother, now *I* have."

"That's why he told you, so that you would not rant at his poor planning. He never said a word to me."

"I'm sorry." Aunt Agatha looked truly remorseful to have blurted it out.

"Don't you see, that could have been Vance."

"Nonsense." She went back to her novel.

A hackney drew up at the house steps and two

figures lurched out. Had they been drinking all this time and come home inebriated?

Though she wanted to run down the stairs to meet them, she restrained her impulse and waited for their explanation. The drawing room door opened, and Tanner supported her brother in, followed by Greeves. Fredrick's clothes were torn and bloodied, and his forehead bore some injury.

"What happened?" Roxanne ran to mop blood from Fredrick's brow. Someone had tied an inadequate handkerchief around it. "Greeves, go get a basin and towels," she ordered.

"We were attacked by footpads in St. James." Tanner wiped his bloody knuckles on his trouser leg and unclenched his hand enough to seat Fredrick on a chair by the table.

"Are you sure they were robbers?" Roxanne asked as she removed the bandage and examined the gash on Fredrick's forehead.

"Of course." Fredrick sounded winded. "Who else would they be?"

"Some of Vance's cohorts. I have to find out what will happen if Fredrick dies before his birthday."

"Oh, give it a rest," her brother complained. "The very thought that he has designs on my life is fantastic. This could have happened to anyone. You should have seen Tanner spring into action. He defeated two of them while I was still struggling up off the paving stones."

"I'm sure a wonderful time was had by all," Lady Agatha said. "Shall I send for the doctor?"

"It's just a cut above my eye and a bruised hand."

"It could have been far worse," Tanner said.

Roxanne paused to stare at her aunt, who seemed to

be extremely calm at the sight of such carnage when a simple social faux pas laid her prostrate. Roxanne shook her head to rid it of the suspicion her aunt was practiced at theatrics and turned to Tanner, cataloging his injuries, the ones that were visible.

"Yes, I know it could have been worse. You could both be dead." She felt her lips tremble as she held her fresh handkerchief to her brother's brow and scanned Tanner's bruised cheek and cut chin. "We should never have dragged you into our affairs. If something happens to you, your mother will be bereft. Holly will never forgive me. I shall never forgive myself."

"Are you actually worried about me?" Tanner asked.

"Of course I'm worried." Roxanne forced her hands to remain steady. "If you had not been with Fredrick, he would have been killed."

Cook came from the kitchen to take charge of bandaging Fredrick's head. Roxanne watched as Tanner hesitated and raked the side of his hand across his chin.

"I see by your silence I am correct," she whispered.

He took her elbow and drew her back toward the window. "Most likely it was just a random attack."

She recognized the lack of conviction in his voice. "I'm sure it was not. Why will no one believe me? What would it cost to be more cautious?"

"Peace of mind. You can't live your life jumping at shadows."

"No one cares that I have no peace." She turned to the window and looked out on the rain-slicked streets.

Tanner moved to stand behind her. "When I came yesterday, I had planned that after I had delivered my news I would offer you the protection of my name."

She managed not to start at this confirmation of her

hope and despair. She turned and saw his face through a blur of tears. "I began to suspect that, after I had driven you away. I am sorry for all my harsh words, but I see now I should never have turned to you and drawn you into this situation."

"If I announce our engagement, Vance will not persecute you. I don't care how long we have to wait."

"If you did that, he would come after you as he did tonight; possibly he would do something to Holly. If nothing else, he will start some gossip to destroy her reputation. You must back away from this family. If Fredrick insists on going to the foundry, I will come with him, armed."

"But I don't want you to feel as though you have to protect your brother. I want to take care of you."

"You can't take care of my mother. She is Vance's prisoner. I have not been able to get in to see her since the night of the ball."

"Has it not occurred to you she may not want to see you?"

Roxanne hesitated, replaying the encounter with her mother in her mind. The embrace had been genuine and had wiped out the three years of estrangement. "She said that we have to talk. She wants to see me. Why else would she come back, unless Vance is afraid to let her out of his sight. That is what it seems. Coming here at this time was Vance's idea, not hers."

"If you imagine so much danger to you and your family, Roxanne, please let me say we are to be married. I can protect Holly."

She stared as his impassioned face. The cut on his chin would leave another scar. She reached her hand up and almost touched the wound, but she had no right.

Tanner was out of her reach for so many reasons. "I love you, Tanner, more than I thought possible for an unromantic sort like me. But I want a partner, not a protector. Besides, I have already said yes to Sir John and probably brought down Vance's wrath on him."

Tanner's face registered his despair. "You accepted Sir John after what I told you?"

"After what you told me, I could not say no to him."

"You will ruin your life."

"Look around you, Tanner. It's too late. My life already stands in ruins."

Tanner left her by the window, hoping that at another time she would not feel so self-sacrificing. He walked home in the rain and let the coolness calm his desperation. What if she was right in her thinking, that Vance planned to murder her brother? If he did nothing to prevent such a tragedy, he was as guilty as Vance. He must keep Fredrick by him or safe at the foundry.

Of course he could not control what the man did the rest of the time. He needed to speak to him and reinforce Rox's warnings. Fredrick might be able to defend himself with a pistol, but taken unawares and alone, he would have no chance.

He also needed to find some chink in Vance's so-perfect armor. The man might just be a talented actor, manipulating everyone for his own benefit. Perhaps Sir John knew something against the villain or could put him in the way of some military companions who did know Vance from the past. It wasn't much, but it was something he could try.

It saddened him that he could do nothing about Roxanne's despair. Could he somehow force his way into the Whitcomb town house and get at the truth? Perhaps news of the attack on her son would be reason enough to push past the servants. Tanner's mind was spinning like a top. He would never get to sleep now.

Chapter Twelve

The next morning after breakfast, Roxanne made an excuse to go to her room. She put on her oldest dress and a poke bonnet to hide her face, then slipped down the backstairs and got a basket from the kitchen, loading it from the pantry. She went to the town house with a story about some preserves sent over by Lady Sherbourne. Roxanne went to the back door, but even there was not admitted. As soon as the butler came to take the present from her, she said she had a note and she must wait for a response.

The butler, a Frenchman, had been called to take the gift and note but advised her not to wait for a reply. When he left with the basket, she went out the kitchen entrance but ducked back in through the coal cellar door, which had never locked properly, and crept up the back stairs. She followed him, moving like a shadow up two flights to the bedrooms. Once he left by the back stairs, she was free to slip out of a linen closet and into her mother's room. She was not in the master suite but a guest chamber. What did that mean?

"Roxanne!" Her mother came and embraced her.

She looked paler by daylight than she had in the candlelit ballroom, and she had lost weight, her cheekbones more prominent than Roxanne recalled. Her fine brown hair now showed strands of gray. The bronze silk dress was one Roxanne's father had given her. Odd that such details about their life together sprang to mind. But her mother's smile made any risk worthwhile.

"You come against Agatha's wishes, I assume."

Roxanne released her to stare at her mother again. "It is not Agatha who conspires to keep us apart but Vance."

"I was afraid of that. What harm does he think we can do by conversing?"

"Fredrick was attacked by footpads in St. James last night. I thought I should tell you he'll be all right."

"Footpads?"

"My question exactly. It's only one day from his birthday. What if something happens to him before he comes of age?"

"I'm not sure. I think Vance would keep charge of your portion."

"What portion? So far as I know, I am penniless."

"I had thought your father put something by for a dowry. Perhaps that is gone as well." Her mother put her hands to her face. "I feel so powerless."

"It doesn't matter. I have accepted a proposal from Sir John Marbrey. I'm to be married, that is, if Vance doesn't kill the poor man."

"I feared our return had ruined your chances. Oh, why did he insist we come?"

"No such thing." Roxanne tried to sound bright. "People have forgotten all about the past. I am a rather infamous hit."

"Truly? I am happy for you, and I did want to see you, but at such a time? Lucius said he had compelling business in London. If I hadn't come with him, he would have come alone."

"Yes, of course. To turn over affairs to Fredrick, if

Vance is legitimate. If not, then to make sure he does not have to turn things over to him."

"This is all my fault. What can I do?"

"Tell Vance you are going to visit Fredrick now that he's been injured. Would Vance prevent it?"

"Lucius thinks I should not go about because of the old gossip."

"We'll discuss it later. Get your things."

"Perhaps Agatha would not want me there. She'll never forgive me for marrying so soon after her brother's death."

"Of course she will." Roxanne was far from feeling guilty about a white lie.

"I was so desperate. I thought that at least if I were off Fredrick's hands he could manage on the allowance Lucius sent him."

"What— We have managed fine. But Vance sent no allowance."

Her mother looked even more stricken. "So that too was a lie."

"You are his prisoner. Why did you agree to marry him?"

"'Tis true there is a footman in the lower hall to prevent my leaving, but I saw no point, before. You won't hate me if I tell you the truth?"

"Of course not. My letters can't have made much sense to you, what with our move and everything."

"Letters." She wiped the tears from her cheeks. "I received no letters."

"I see. We leased the main house to Vance for three years. Surely he told you. We needed the money to buy things for Fredrick's work."

"No, he never mentioned it. But where do you live.

In London?"

"At the gatekeeper's cottage with Cook."

"It's so small."

"It has the stable for a workshop nearby. Don't worry, really. Now, are you all right?"

"Yes, of course." She blotted her face again and turned away as she said it.

Roxanne didn't believe that either.

"I can understand you being overwrought, but you went away with Vance, then married him a year later, almost exactly as though you had to wait. Why did you do it? We would have taken care of you."

Her mother turned to her with trembling lips. "To keep him from marrying you."

"Ahh!" Roxanne felt the breath wrenched from her body as a chill ran through her. She would have been sixteen then. All this time she had thought of her mother as being weak, yet she had put herself in the way of a villain to keep her daughter out of his reach. "I should have guessed. Come with me now." She reached for her hand and grasped it, shocked at how chill it felt. "I sneaked in. Surely you can sneak out."

"That would be unwise. I still stand between you and Vance. I must continue to do so. I shall kill him if I have to, in order to keep you safe."

Roxanne was mesmerized by her mother's face which now had a strength she had never seen there before. "Don't go that far. I will find a way to rescue you. Just give me a day. Come to think of it, a day is all I have." She embraced her mother before she crept out the way she had come.

****

"What if this solicitor still refuses to see Rox?"

Harding asked. The carriage jerked to a halt in Grey's Inn Road, and he helped Holly and Roxanne out. "You may walk the horses," he told the driver.

"That's what you're here for, to break down the door," Holly said.

Roxanne sighed. "Let's hope we don't need anything so drastic as a broken door." Though she was glad for Harding's presence, she wished Holly would have agreed to stay home. Still, it was Holly who had convinced the captain to come.

"Could you break a door if you had to?" Holly asked.

Harding chuckled. "Depends on the door."

They trudged up the stairs to the landing where the clerk held audience.

"Miss Whitcomb to see Mr. Fenster."

"'E's not in."

"I have an appointment."

"Things change."

"Made a liar out of you, has he?" Roxanne asked. "This time we will wait in his office. He has to come back sooner or later."

Harding restrained the clerk as Roxanne advanced on the door and flung it open to discover a spectacled young man sitting at a desk.

"Sir, if I were a man, I would call you coward to your face and challenge you," she shouted.

"Who are you?" the man asked.

"Roxanne Whitcomb. I believe your father was our solicitor, and I suspect he made a deal with my guardian to cheat me and my brother out of our inheritance."

"Those are serious charges." He rose and placed his hands on the pile of papers on the desk.

Roxanne marched up to the desk. "Murder is a serious matter."

"Who are these two?"

"My dear friend Miss Tanner, and Harding of the Bow Street Runners."

Harding rolled his gaze toward Holly, and she grinned.

"'ere now! Was there a need for all this?" the clerk asked as he came to close the door.

"Apparently, yes, Goff. I have told you not to drive my clients away. Now go get the records for the Whitcomb estate."

Goff shut the door behind him and reappeared some minutes later with a portfolio.

"What is it you wish to know?" Fenster asked.

"The terms of my father's will."

"Here is the document. You may peruse it at your leisure."

Roxanne sat down and read. "But this is not his handwriting and certainly not his signature. Where is his real will?"

"That is the only one in the box."

"So Vance has stolen everything, including my father's life. But why? If Father was done up, why would Vance seek control of a debt-ridden estate?"

"Who told you that?" Fenster asked.

"Everyone. I'm as poor as a church mouse."

"No, when you marry, you will have an income of five thousand pounds a year."

Roxanne sat back in the chair, glad that she was sitting when she received this news. "How can that be? We were told we could not keep up the estate. We have been living in the gatehouse."

"Told by whom?"

"Lucius Vance."

"He is your guardian by the terms of this will, but he was to have paid you an allowance to keep up the estate."

"As mother said, but he didn't. He paid a small amount of rent on the estate. So to keep his crimes secret, he not only has to kill Fredrick but me and Mother, as well."

"I am so sorry. I only just took over the whole business from my father. I had no idea."

"How did your father die?" Holly asked.

Fenster was startled into replying. "It was…a carriage accident."

Harding and Roxanne exchanged glances.

"Murdered," Holly said. "Vance will stop at nothing."

"If you all will wait here, I'll send Goff for the magistrate."

Roxanne was pleased he took her seriously. "You don't think Goff could be implicated?"

"Oh, my God."

They rushed to the door to find the safe open and Goff gone.

Fenster shook his head. "I have much to answer for."

"Someone does," Roxanne said, "but it isn't you."

"Lucky you employed a runner."

"That was just a ruse," Harding replied. "I wish I *were* from Bow Street. But I will go get the magistrate if you give me his direction. In the meantime, you all can sort out the list of charges. May as well get the wheels of justice rolling."

****

Tanner started as he entered his salon looking for his

sister and found Roxanne there instead. She was wearing a becoming green dimity dress, but everything she wore became her. She was that sort of woman who made clothes look good rather than relying on clothes to set off her looks.

But at the moment those looks were wan and worried, as befit her situation. It was not done for a young lady without escort to be shown into a gentleman's drawing room. He knew that much. She glanced at him in abstraction as though she had other things on her mind.

"Is something the matter?" Tanner asked, not used to seeing her so unsure.

"I came to call on your mother for advice. She and Holly are expected back soon."

"I should leave you, then. But you will be seeing her tomorrow night when you all go to the Meisners' ball."

"That may be too late."

Tanner had felt so beaten up emotionally he had announced he did not mean to escort them to the theater tonight. That's what Captain Harding was for, but he felt the urge to go back upstairs and change into evening clothes. Of course it was not even dinner time, and Roxanne was not in evening dress. Perhaps she did not plan to go out, not if she was this distressed.

"What is it? He came to sit beside her and took her hands. They were cold to the touch, as though she'd had some great shock.

"Are you quite sure you want to hear this?"

"I would not have asked if I did not care."

"I sneaked through the kitchens at our town house and got in to see Mother. She did want to talk to me. She said something about the allowances Lucius sends to

Fredrick and me. I spoke to Fredrick and he's never gotten a penny. And I've just been to see our solicitor."

"Alone? Do you think that was wise?"

Rox snatched her hands back. "Yes. It was a good idea when I had it and an even better one now that I know Vance has been cheating us all. There is more to it than that."

"You always imagine the worst." He was beginning to feel queasy about his recent ridicule of her suspicions. If she was right about one thing, possibly she had guessed right on others.

"Let me spit back at you your recent apology. 'You were right,' you said. And now I have more to go on than a hunch. I have a huge discrepancy. Mother was not told the estate was leased for three years."

"A wise move. Fredrick can't afford it yet, but when he can, it will be waiting for him."

"If he's still alive. I wondered why Vance leased it and never came there once they were married. It's because he does not want us to talk to her."

"Are you sure that is the case? Have you spoken to Vance?"

"I spoke to my mother, and that is quite enough proof of his villainy. Captain Harding went with us today, so we did get to speak to the solicitor."

"Us? Did you drag my innocent sister to a solicitor's office?"

"I couldn't very well keep her away, considering she was the one to convince Harding to aid me. Why do you always do that?"

"What?" Tanner drew back at her attack. Any time he admonished Rox, she always managed to beat back with some mistake of his own that made him forget what she had done wrong.

"Disparage her as though she cannot think for herself. She may be innocent, but she's smart and agile enough to have stayed ahead of the pack of hounds you set to hunt her."

Tanner felt the blood drain from his face. Rox had spoken to him plainly before about the way he treated his sister, but never in these terms.

"Is that how it seems to you?"

"Yes, to any woman of intelligence. We must step lively to stay away from the worst of men, stay one step ahead of the fortune hunters, and try to figure out if there is one good heart among all the men in London."

He felt an internal struggle, replaying in his own mind all the worst things he had said to his sister.

"Very well. I will listen to her and won't patronize her again."

"I hope to be around to make sure you keep that vow."

"Why wouldn't you be?"

"If Vance is trying to kill my brother, how safe do you think my life is, or my mother's?"

Tanner felt rocked to his foundations. Was everything he thought he knew about these people a fabrication? He had met Vance twice, and though he didn't like him, he could find no fault. Vance had not looked down on him for being in trade, but was that any standard for measuring character?

Lucius Vance was a soldier, so he had killed and possibly was hardened to it. It was no easier to shrug off a threat to Rox than it was to Holly. Yet he knew Rox was not helpless. Still, he must do something to make her believe he wasn't just one of the well-meaning but impotent men who did much harm by doing nothing.

"I'm sorry. I had no right to speak so plainly, for I do believe you are a good man, but women have so few rights or choices that I cannot bear to see Holly trying to choose between the lesser of many evils rather than a man who will make her truly happy."

"I have always shielded her from the world."

"Which makes it doubly hard when you thrust her suddenly into it with the abjuration to choose a man, any man with a title, and have done with it. I suppose that's so you can get on with your affairs. I mean your business affairs. So bloodless, compared to real life."

"Perhaps you think my life has been easy. Father never wanted me in the business. Even if he walked in here today he would do nothing but criticize."

"Much like you criticize Holly or your mother or any of their charitable efforts?"

"I let them do as they will."

"But you get this look on your face. I have seen it."

"Work is the thing that makes us all."

"And yet you aspire to the *ton*. Stop pursuing dead fashion and set your own, but temper your ethic with compassion. There are many too ill or hungry to work."

"I am tired of being lectured by women." He got up and strode toward the door, then recalled it was his house and he could not evade her plain truths by leaving.

"Yes, that inferior species, long on compassion but short of brains. I see my estimation of you was premature. I really thought you had changed."

"Do you think that's your mission, to change me?"

"Absolutely not. I think it is your mission to change yourself. I take responsibility only for my own actions. It is crystal clear to me, now, that you cannot be mended."

"Only one thing is crystal clear to me now. You never had any interest in me, only in my money."

"What are you talking about? I did want you to invest in Fredrick's inventions, so I could not in good conscience let you court me until that was settled. I'm sorry I turned you down. If I wanted your money, I would have accepted you when you proposed. Now I see that it was wise of me to keep you at arm's length, for the sake of your family."

"Answer me. Do you care about me at all?" He ran his hands through his hair.

"Of course I do. I love you. Why would I rant at you if I didn't?"

"I really don't know. I have never met anyone like you."

He watched her struggle to voice her terms and conditions for caring about him.

"You are Holly's brother, and I want so much not to lose her friendship, but you set too high a price on yourself."

"What price? I would have given you everything. I offered you the protection of my name."

"That's not quite the same thing. You offered me everything except what I needed—your trust in my judgment. Now I find that Vance has registered a fake will with the solicitor. Father never meant for Vance to be our guardian. Not only that, I think Vance killed my father."

"The solicitor agrees with you?"

"He sent Harding for the magistrate. You patted me on the head and assured me my brother's life is not in danger. That kind of protection I do not need." Rox got up and pulled her shawl about her.

"Perhaps Vance did try to cheat you, but he would never dare murder. Your brother can take care of himself. Didn't he kill that highwayman on Houndslow Heath?"

"Oh, yes, the highwayman?" Her voice echoed in the otherwise quiet room.

"I think I should let *him* tell you about that."

"Perhaps he may live to do so."

"How could you not realize my interest went beyond your brother's affairs?"

"Because you never said anything. I have been dumped before, and it's not a pleasant experience to think someone cares and then discover he was only a very good actor. I wanted to put it off as long as possible, hating you."

"If one of your calf loves…"

"It was Lord Wainwright, to be specific. The day after Father was killed, Wainwright disappeared from my life and refused to answer my letters. When I next saw him, he was courting one of the Cavendish girls and he looked at me as though I were invisible."

"How was I supposed to know all this unless you told me?"

"To what purpose? You said it yourself, I have no talent for these false games everyone plays." She pulled the strings taut on her bag. "No need to see me out. I know my way by now."

"Rox, wait."

"Tell your mother I will ask her advice tomorrow."

"Am I no use to you?"

"Not when you don't believe me."

"If I had any proof Vance was doing this, I would call him out."

"A white knight is not what I need right now. I had much rather you smashed in his face in your usual manner. But even that would require some proof, apparently, and I intend to get it."

Tanner let her have the last word and followed her to the door to make sure she had a footman for escort. Then he went to the study to brood. He had spoken to Fredrick about Roxanne's suspicions, and her brother had laughed about them. But this was different. She had a solicitor who agreed with her.

He should ignore Fredrick's words of comfort and call on Vance. He couldn't just walk into the house and smash in his face, as Rox suggested, but he might be able to strangle the truth out of him.

Then he recalled he had a solicitor as well, and he had asked him for confirmation of Sir John's state of affairs. Tomorrow he would also ask him to see what gossip he could pick up in the inns of court about Vance and his doings.

****

Roxanne was pleased that for once Fredrick stayed home that evening. She thought it was more because his head ached than that he had heeded her fears. She kept checking in the book room to make sure he wasn't about to sneak out. The pretense of getting something to read could not serve her more than three or four times.

"Have you a new dress for the ball tomorrow night?"

"It's no use, Freddy. I don't want to go to the ball tomorrow if Tanner is going to be there. He tricked me. He wasn't interested in your inventions at first, just in seducing me."

Her brother gave her that impatient stare of his as he looked up from the drawings he'd spread on the book room table. "I'm sure that cannot be right. Still, I must discuss this with him, since I believe he is genuinely interested in you."

Roxanne gave him a punch in the shoulder that made him grin.

"I didn't mean I would discuss his seduction of you, of course, so don't get that look."

"What look?" Roxanne demanded, knowing her anger showed in her face.

"As though you want me to call him out."

"He wanted to court me, and I never realized. Why didn't he say something?"

"Then you do care about him?"

"Of course I do. I didn't presume to think about it then."

"Or you were afraid to," Fredrick suggested with a sad smile.

"It doesn't matter. The things we said to each other... It was much worse than parting from Wainwright. *He* just never spoke to me again. I read Tanner out about his treatment of Holly. For that he will never forgive me."

"Perhaps all is not lost. Would you wish him to court you?"

"I don't know. He is the most aggravating man I have ever met. We fight like ferrets in a sack every time we talk."

"You used to say that about me, and then Wainwright. My dear levelheaded sister, if you don't know, you must be moonstruck."

"More like thunderstruck. Wait until I tell you what our guardian has been up to. But first I want to hear about the highwayman you killed."

Fredrick had the grace to blush. "So bloodthirsty. I could hardly let him rob the female passengers, since two of them looked needier than us."

"Don't you see? Vance might have sent him. Then we have the attack last night. Your life is in danger."

"But that defies all reason. You can't blame everything on Vance."

"Just because you cannot work out that there is a plot doesn't mean there isn't one. I saw the solicitor today, and he agrees the will he has is a forgery. Certainly Vance has been cheating us. We are not poor, the way he says."

"The solicitor agrees with you about Vance trying to kill me?"

"He agrees for a fact Vance is embezzling from us. The magistrate is investigating. I have convinced our solicitor your life is in danger."

"I can see I will have to visit him without delay. I am sorry I was so caught up in my work I ignored your fears."

"You will be careful, then?"

"We'll let the law take care of Vance. I don't think he would dare try to do away with me now."

Roxanne went to her chamber with an evil headache, but she felt she had finally made a dent in Fredrick's complaisance. He at least agreed to go visit the solicitor, but he did not take the danger to his life seriously. She didn't even want to talk to him about Mother. She had championed her and made excuses for no letters long after Fredrick had washed his hands of her.

Against her romantic problem she could make no headway. She loved Tanner and would much rather have become engaged to him than to Sir John, but she had given her word and would not back down on that.

She felt sorry for the older man who had proposed when Tanner was angry with her. Sympathy was not sufficient reason for marriage, but she had just as much honor as a man. She would not cry off, but she must warn Sir John of the dangers Vance presented.

Then she recalled that she had far more serious problems than marrying someone she didn't really love. She had to figure out how to rescue her mother. Fredrick had not believed her when she'd told him that Mother was a prisoner. He certainly had his doubts that their solicitor was calling in a magistrate to prosecute Vance. All he cared about was the casting he was ready to do the next day, as though nothing mattered but his inventions.

She had to devise a way to rescue her mother on her own.

Perhaps Vance would be arrested soon enough to solve all her problems, but she placed as little trust in the wheels of justice as she did in men. They still had to get a warrant. She must be ready to spring into action herself.

Chapter Thirteen

Aunt Agatha spent the morning planning Roxanne's trousseau and immediate future. She was to have all new finery in spite of just getting a dozen new gowns. Agatha could now take her to the Meisners' ball that night with a good conscience, since Roxanne was engaged.

She was puzzled by Roxanne's lack of enthusiasm for her plans but happily went off to order fabric while Roxanne stayed home and waited for word about the warrant for Vance. She had sneaked into the town house once and should be able to do so again, but how could she convince her mother to leave? Even if she got Vance arrested, there was still Ian Stone to deal with. At least Fredrick had promised to see the solicitor as soon as possible.

Roxanne had worn a path in the carpet, pacing the morning room. It was nearly noon and still no solutions had suggested themselves by the time Tanner was announced. With difficulty, she composed herself, shaking the creases out of her green striped morning gown as she went to greet him. It was not the thing for young ladies to receive gentlemen alone in the morning room, but she hoped Tanner did not realize that.

"Please sit down, sir. This time I owe you an apology for my rant about your family affairs. I had no more right to intrude, even if I am Holly's best friend, than you had to advise me about my prospects."

"And I came to apologize for dumping such awful news on your yesterday." Tanner took a seat across from her in front of the fireplace.

"I can scarcely believe it. But Aunt Agatha has been gone for hours, and that makes me queasy." Roxanne looked up at the mantel clock. "She can't have been ordering fabric all this time, so perhaps she is listening to gossip."

"I fear it's true. My solicitor confirmed it. I went to your town house and could not gain admittance. They claim Vance is not home."

"And short of pushing past the servants, you cannot know if they are lying.

"I will find him and wring the truth out of him."

"No matter. The die is cast. A horrible way to put it, but gambling cant does not make me shudder now that I know my father did not game his fortune away."

"Your solicitor changed your opinion?"

"When so many investors were selling out of the funds on the eve of Waterloo, Father bought stock. He made a fortune."

"Then why would he kill himself?"

"That's the point, Tanner. I'm sure he didn't. I recall that Vance arrived on the twentieth with bad news. His investments were wiped out since he sold late. Father shook his head and said not to worry. They sat up drinking after we went to bed. Then I heard that horrible shot. I tried to get into the library, but it was locked. Later Vance said he did not want me to witness the sight, but I now know he needed time to sober up and write the fake will."

"Can you prove any of this?"

"I think all of it, now that the solicitor has told me

what he knows."

"I have let you down. If I had championed you at the solicitor's office, he may have seen you the first time you called. I was so caught up in what I thought were my responsibilities I ignored your very real plight and almost married my sister to a bounder."

"I am glad you realized it in time, for Holly's sake."

"I talked to her—rather, I listened for a change. She doesn't want any of them."

"And?"

"And I told her she doesn't have to accept any of them. There's always next year."

"Tanner, that is wonderful!" She wasn't sure how, but she found herself in his arms, hugging him, but then she recollected where they were. She drew back to look at him, and he bent and kissed her.

She returned the kiss tentatively, but recalled her situation and stared at him with her hands clutching his lapels and probably ruining them. "I just remembered I am engaged."

"I am aware of it." His arms still held her close.

"To someone else," she reminded him.

"I have come to my senses too late. I was trying to do the right thing, but my course is more littered with mistakes that a novice's weaving."

"Your missteps can be mended. You have made a start, but I have given my word."

"There was a time I would have chided you about a woman's word, but that would be unfair. Your honor is just as important to you as mine is to me."

The door cracked open, and they leaped apart. Sir John was announced and strode into the room still carrying a riding crop.

"Miss Whitcomb, I have come to tell you that I must withdraw my offer of marriage. I find that the son and daughter-in-law I trusted have ruined me, and I am, in good conscience, in no position to take a wife."

Roxanne swallowed and stared at him, this kindly man who'd been willing to take her when no one else would. She glanced at Tanner, and he looked away, wincing at some inner hurt.

"Fortune or no, it matters not to me," she finally said.

Sir John came and took her hand. "You are a dear girl to say so, but I cannot allow you to throw yourself away on me. Surely someone else will offer for you."

"You are a man of honor, sir. I must tell you that our situations have been strangely reversed. It appears my father was not ruined after all and that I shall have an income that would support us."

"I am indeed happy for you, but I must find my own way out of this mess, so I feel compelled to withdraw my offer. No blame will attach to you. I shall see to that. Everyone knows my affairs now and will understand."

"But how? How can everyone know so suddenly?"

"I'm not sure, but it doesn't matter."

"Was it my guardian who did this to you?"

"It was only a matter of time. I should not have been so blind. For now, I must go see my solicitors." He kissed her lightly on the forehead and strode from the room.

"Now *that* is a gentleman," she whispered.

Tanner came to stand behind her so close she could feel his breath upon her neck.

"It wasn't me," he said.

"What?" She turned to face him.

"It wasn't me who told about his affairs."

"I never thought it was. What just happened here?"

"You had a chance to reverse your decision, but you chose honor above love."

"Did I? I was only thinking how much more he needed me than you do."

"Still, you chose him rather than me. Will you never think of what you need, what you want?"

"I was thinking of that. How could I have lived with myself if I had been the one who abandoned him?"

"Many women do make such decisions without regret."

"I am not many women. I am me, too much like my father for my own good. If you can't accept that, I'm sorry." She wasn't sure what his intense look meant, but she did not find out, since Aunt Agatha burst into the room with news of Sir John's disgrace.

She reclined on the divan fanning herself and castigating the older man until Roxanne told her Sir John had broken the engagement. She wasn't sure from her aunt's hysterical laughter if she was happy or sadly insane about that. At any rate, Tanner slipped from the room before she could speak to him again.

Were they never to settle anything? But did she want to accept him when her whole life was still in an uproar? She would far rather come to him without such baggage. And if she was honest with herself, she did want to vanquish her own dragon, in this case.

She went to her room, where her celestial blue ball gown was laid out along with her cloak, gloves, and slippers. Such fripperies when her heart was breaking into pieces. Well, if Tanner couldn't stomach a wife with a sense of honor, he could just go marry one of the debutantes and ruin himself. She pulled her trunk from under the bed and got out her father's dueling pistol. It was the lonely mate to the one that had killed him. She was never sure what they had done with that one, but she'd found this one in the library in its usual place.

She carefully loaded it in preparation for tomorrow's expedition. Or if she could escape the ball tonight, perhaps she could accomplish her task this evening. The ball was the sort of place Vance would go without taking her mother.

The more she thought about it, the more she saw tonight as a golden opportunity to break her mother free. Possibly she could slip away unnoticed. If she mistook not, the Meisner town house was only one square over from her father's town house. She changed, slid the pistol into the pocket of her black velvet cloak, and carried it downstairs.

****

Tanner drove to the foundry, to discover that the casting had been poured and two workmen were watching over it. Fredrick had gone home to change for the ball tonight. Tanner wasn't at all sure he wanted to go, to see Rox there and hear the unkind gossip about her and Sir John. In fact, he had told his mother he was not going. What might have been a triumph for Rox would now be another evening of torture.

There would be plenty of tongues who claimed she had jilted the old man because of his reverses. And she had dragged Holly into the sad affair of her father and his finances, or rather Holly had intruded into her affairs. True friends did that kind of thing for you. He had been less than a friend to Rox and meant to make it up to her.

He also meant to marry her if she would have him. He decided to go home and change for the Meisners' ball.

He'd be damned if he'd propose on the dance floor, but surely he could get her alone for a moment, even if he had to carry her off to a secluded room.

He'd been waiting in his drawing room twenty minutes, rehearsing his proposal, before he realized the house was absurdly quiet. Then he recalled they were all supposed to gather at Lady Sherbourne's and leave from there in her carriage. No matter. He would simply walk. If he knew those two girls, they would be comparing dresses for many minutes before they left for the ball. And even if he missed them he could hire a hackney.

On the way out of the house, he checked with his butler and confirmed that Fredrick had come for Holly and his mother some time ago. It was a fine cool night, and the walk cleared his head. When he arrived at Lady Sherbourne's and was shown into the drawing room, only Rox and her aunt were waiting.

"Where are Holly and Mother?"

"We were just wondering the same thing," Rox said. "Fredrick went to fetch them."

"Could they have had an accident?" Lady Sherbourne asked.

"I suppose there is more than one route from here to there. Perhaps I missed them."

He heard carriage wheels in the street, and Roxanne stepped to the window. "There is our carriage. Shall we go out and save them the steps?"

He helped them into their cloaks, but as they started down the outside steps, his mother leaned out of the carriage window.

"Spencer! Thank God. Holly and Fredrick have been kidnapped!"

"What?" Tanner shouted.

"A carriage cut us off, sir," the coachman said, "and while I was struggling with the team, three men came up on us and dragged them away. They knocked Mr. Whitcomb out. It was a trap."

"I told him to pursue them, Spencer, but the press of traffic hampered us."

"Which way did they go?" Roxanne demanded.

"East."

A hackney stopped and Harding got out. "Shall I hang onto this carriage? Do we have enough seats in the coach?"

Roxanne ran to him. "Holly's been abducted, and Fredrick with her."

"What? But why?"

"I should have remembered wealth makes her a target," Tanner said. "Mother, can you go inside with Lady Sherbourne and wait for us here. We must rouse the watch and try to find them."

"We will wait here," her aunt said as she helped Tanner's mother up the steps.

Roxanne grabbed the carriage door as Tanner was about to vault through it. "I'm coming with you."

"I think you should stay with the other women."

"Not a chance."

"Of course Rox is coming," Harding said, helping her into the carriage.

"Drive to the docks," she commanded. "Father's yacht, the *Silverloo*, is anchored somewhere there."

"I saw it. I know where it is." Harding climbed up with the driver and took the reins rather than waste time giving directions.

"Are you sure?" Tanner asked.

"Vance has taken them. He plans to kill Fredrick and

dump his body at sea. I'm not sure what he plans for Holly, but we must find them now."

When the carriage stopped, it was between two warehouses with the quay barely in sight. Harding flung himself down and opened the door.

"They're still anchored here. They have to wait for the tide. But we need more help. My ship is nearby. I propose leaving you here to keep watch while I go to get reinforcements. Tanner, you might discreetly try to engage that lighter to carry us out to the yacht."

"If your superiors find out what you are doing, you could lose your rank," Tanner warned.

"What does that matter if I lose Holly?" Harding mounted the box again and took the reins.

Tanner pulled Rox back against the wall. "It's Captain Harding she's in love with."

"See how much he loves her?" she asked.

"Harding? I always thought him simply reliable."

"Just what one wants in a husband."

"We shouldn't have let you come," Tanner said. "This could be dangerous."

"When we do find Holly, she may need me."

"That's true, but what if all your tenuous guesses are wrong? Then Harding is ruined and we have still lost them."

"We have to do this." She peeked around the corner of the building. "They're on that ship. I can feel it."

"How?"

She didn't answer him for a moment because she didn't understand it herself. The smell of the harbor, the offending slap of water against the sides of the yacht, all spelled a hopelessness at variance with her childish memories of the *Silverloo*. Her father had won it in a card game, hence the name, and kept it at Exeter for fishing. But the ship looked dirty and in ill repair now. She knew it had been besmirched by Vance's evil.

"I have an instinct for guessing what people are thinking." She pressed her back against the brick warehouse beside him. "If I were as evil as Vance, it's what I would do."

"Very well, I have learned to trust your judgment."

"If I'm wrong, what harm have I done?"

"Introduced my sister to a preventive officer."

"A captain of the Coast Guard. Besides, you just told her she need not marry to please you."

"You are right."

"I am right about this as well. If Vance gets them out of port, I fear for both their lives. Are you going to hire that boatman?"

"Stay here."

Tanner was happy to see Harding back in twenty minutes and with a dozen stout fellows packed into the carriage or riding on top. Now they would know if Rox was right. For all their sakes, he hoped so. He had no alternate plan, no idea at all where his sister could be.

"Only two guards posted, and they look half drunk," Harding said. "They must be confident they have gotten away with this. Afraid there isn't room for you in the boat, Rox. Stay with the coachman. Come along, Tanner. Don't worry. We do this sort of raid all the time."

Tanner breathed a sigh of relief as Rox stepped back from the edge of the quay.

"No problem," Rox replied. "I'll cover you from here."

"Cover us?" Tanner asked as Harding pushed him down into the boat. "What does that mean?"

"Don't worry," Harding advised.

As they were rowing away, Rox produced a long-barreled pistol from her cloak and rested it on her forearm.

"Now I'm worried." Tanner glanced at Harding to get his reaction.

"Give over. Would she bring such a weapon if she didn't know how to use it?"

"I don't know. Sometimes I think I don't know her at all."

"You underestimate her, just as you did Holly." Harding stood and held onto the mast in the small space left in the lighter.

"You're probably right. Have you any authority for what we are doing?"

"Absolutely none. There is some risk in any profession. If, as I suspect, the ship is also carrying French brandy, hidden and not taxed, then I'm home free. If, as I fear, they have Holly and Fredrick on board but no brandy, then I'll be reprimanded but not court martialed."

"If neither are true?"

Harding shrugged. "Apologize and hope for the best."

"You're hanging your career on Rox's guess."

"It's mine to risk. And you are here, after all."

Tanner shook his head. "I have learned what comes of not listening to her."

"The crew probably won't be armed with pistols. If they were, they'd get drunk and shoot each other."

"They're speaking some foreign language, like those footpads who attacked Fredrick and me in St. James," Tanner whispered. "They have a foreign crew."

"It's French. What of it? You speak French, don't you?" Harding asked.

"Seems to be a missing chink in my education."

Harding gave him a look of reprimand, then drew out and cocked his pistol.

Chapter Fourteen

Roxanne was glad for her black cloak as she worked her way along the quay until she had a good view of the deck of the *Silverloo*. She climbed a stack of crates to get a better angle, much to the distress of the coachman, yet he obeyed her orders and stayed at the horses' heads in case they should have to make a quick getaway.

No one on the ship seemed to notice the feathered oars of the lighter as it was pulled toward the yacht. But perhaps in the smuggling trade the arrival of small boats in the night was only to be expected. The lamps swinging on the yacht in no way lit the dark sides of the vessel. Harding's crew seemed to swarm up the sides of the ship as silently as snakes.

The boarding party surprised the sleepy watch, and Roxanne thought the Frenchmen seemed inclined to give up, but Stone stepped on deck and started to shout at Harding. Stone was drunk himself, so Tanner had no trouble disarming him. When Harding took one of his men and went toward the cabin to search, Roz saw Stone draw another pistol out of his waistband and point it at Tanner, who was helping to disarm the crew of their knives and cutlasses.

She shouted a warning but no one heard her, so she took aim and fired, knocking Stone to the deck. His other pistol slithered toward Tanner, who grabbed it. Tanner looked over at her—in accusation, she thought. Then he smiled and she fell in love with him all over again.

She had not brought the kit to reload. Foolish of her. So there was nothing she could do for the long minutes of the search except listen to Stone whimpering and cursing to the point where she wished they would gag him. "If you don't expect to be fired upon, then you shouldn't try to shoot someone in the back," she yelled.

Only the coachman heard her, and he gave a chuckle.

Then she saw Fredrick being led onto the deck, supported by both Harding and a crewman. There was blood all over his shirt and he looked pale, but he was alive. Half her fears were relieved as Harding got the keys to his manacles from Stone. It appeared she hadn't given Stone a mortal wound, but he was holding one arm.

"You attacked my vessel," Stone shouted.

"You abducted an Englishman with the intention of murdering him," Tanner said. "Where is my sister?"

"I don't know what you're talking about."

Fredrick's head came up. "I was knocked out. I thought I was the only one taken."

"My crew is searching the vessel from stem to stern," Harding said. "If she is harmed in any way, you won't live to face trial."

"Hold him here," Tanner said. "I'll go below and search for myself."

Harding shouted in French the punishment for attacking a preventive officer, and the French crew froze. He also held a pistol to the head of Stone, demanding to know where Holly was. The Frenchmen waited for Stone to give her up, but he shook his head.

Tanner saw the splintered door to the cabin and no trace of his sister. This was where Fredrick had been held, but why keep them separate? He heard a thumping and went to the built-in chest under the aft windows.

It was locked, but he broke the catch with the butt of the pistol and found Holly bound and gagged inside. He lifted her out with tears in his eyes. Thank God for Rox and her wild notions.

"Are you truly all right?" He pulled the gag off and worked the ropes off her bruised wrists.

"Yes, what about Fredrick?" she asked, breathless. "They knocked him senseless."

"He seems well enough to walk."

"What would they have done to us?"

"Don't think about it." He hugged her to him and picked her up in his arms. "I'm taking you home to Mother."

Harding was raising the pistol to deliver a blow to the recalcitrant Stone when Holly gave a small shriek of joy at sight of him.

"James, you came for me?"

"We all came," Harding said. He let Stone slump to the deck with a painful thump.

Tanner was sure he would have embraced Holly if not for so many witnesses to the rescue.

"Rox is on the quay, probably reloading her pistol," Harding informed her.

"What true friends you all are." Holly hugged Harding in spite of the witnesses.

"Captain Harding, sir, we found brandy bottles under a layer of cordwood ballast, hundreds of them, with no stamp."

"Good work, Lieutenant. Lock the crew in the hold that doesn't have the brandy and tell them if they make a sound they will be bound and gagged. Set a watch to catch any buyers who might row out. I'll report all in the morning and send you a relief guard."

Roxanne waited impatiently for the lighter to bring the others back to the quay. Before Holly let herself be lowered to the boat in the bosun's chair, she went straight up to Stone, who had just struggled to his feet with bound hands, and kicked him in the chins hard enough to topple him. The British crew chuckled at this. Harding's pistol was knocked askew but was replaced by the one Tanner held to Stone's head.

"Drag this scum into the boat," Harding shouted. "He has more to answer for than smuggling."

"What?" Stone protested.

"Kidnapping two British citizens."

"Now you are kidnapping me," Stone protested weakly.

"You're under arrest," Harding said. "Make no mistake about that."

"You don't want to do that. Think of the scandal."

Harding cocked the pistol. "I could care less about scandal. But you are right. Perhaps it would be better if you were accidentally shot while attempting to escape."

Roxanne thought she could see a sheen of sweat on Stone's face in the lamplight.

"But Vance will tell everyone. Little Miss Holly will have no reputation left. You'd be better off letting me go."

"You going to gossip from your cell?" Harding asked. "Be my guest."

"He may be right," Tanner said. "Holly could be ruined in society."

"As if I care," Holly said. "I'm marrying Captain Harding. I want this man arrested and punished. I shall testify against him myself if I have to."

"You've become remarkably decisive, my dear," Harding said.

Tanner laughed as he helped Holly into the bosun's chair.

Roxanne was pleased he had unclenched. He truly was a hero now, and he had not disdained her help. The next time he asked her to marry him, she would say yes. She just hoped it was after she rescued her mother.

When they arrived at Lady Sherbourne's house, the comment that stopped them in their tracks was her aunt's astonished, "Roxanne, you've ruined your dress." They all burst out laughing as Holly looked down at her own tattered white gown.

"I must go change. Come, Holly. I should have a dress that will fit you."

Fredrick laughed. "If you are still planning on going to that ball, Holly, I'm afraid I'm not up to it."

Agatha stood. "We must go, all of us, to show that nothing untoward has happened."

"We are pressing charges, but no one need know the circumstances," Tanner said. "Yes, let us go and dance with wild abandon, except Fredrick who was hit over the head yet again." He was standing by his mother's chair with his hand on her shoulder.

"Be careful of her, Spencer. Bring her back safely."

"I shall stay here with your dear mother," Fredrick announced, "until my head stops spinning."

The girls went upstairs to find new gowns to wear.

"Was she harmed?" his mother asked Tanner.

"Her wrists are bruised. Stone was too drunk to attempt anything worse. I'm afraid Rox was right," he whispered. "Stone was planning on dumping Fredrick overboard."

"Probably at Vance's request," Fredrick said. "Why didn't I listen to Rox? She's always right."

"I wish Harding had been able to come home with us," Tanner said. "He does enjoy dancing, and the girls will miss him as a partner."

"Where is Harding?" asked Lady Sherbourne.

"He's busy delivering Stone to jail and writing up all his reports. However, he does plan to call on me tomorrow—well, Holly and me."

"He helped save her life, Spencer. I will not object to the marriage in the slightest."

"I see now how I have erred in many matters, not valuing Harding being one of them."

His mother smiled. "Good. I knew you could change."

Tanner shook his head. "Imagine Rox putting that ball through Stone's arm."

Fredrick squinted at him as he held a cold compress to the back of his neck. "Rox said he was going to shoot you."

"I did not realize that. Such unplumbed depths your sister has. Catch me doubting anything she says from now on."

****

Roxanne looked down at her cream gown with scallops of lace, the one she had worn to Holly's ball. She liked it much better than the wispy blue one that was now muddy and torn. As Roxanne had suspected, Vance was attending the Meisners' ball and her mother was not. He would not be surprised to see her here, since she had not been one of his victims. Or was that true? What if the abductors thought they were taking Fredrick and her, but got Holly by mistake? She shuddered at the thought they might have killed Holly in her stead. It was enough that she felt responsible for her father's death. Another innocent life on her conscience would have driven her mad.

She made sure she got Vance's attention early and watched him watching her as she made small talk with her aunt while Holly took part in a country dance. She wanted to make sure she was watching Vance when he noticed Holly.

"What are you doing?" Tanner asked.

Roxanne jumped a little at the sound of his voice, but the shivers he sent along her arms were not ones of fear. "Trying to see if Holly's presence surprises Vance," she replied.

Vance glanced up then and noticed Tanner's sister but did not seem surprised other than to scan the room and ascertain that Tanner was present. Or perhaps he was making sure that Fredrick was not.

"He may have heard already that his scheme did not work," Tanner said.

Rox frowned. "If that were true, he would be packing, not here drinking. It is possible that in taking Holly, Stone acted on his own initiative and planned to keep her for himself. If you were Vance and kidnapping someone with his death in mind, would you want an extra witness?"

"No, but I have a difficult time putting myself in that position."

"You do not empathize well. A villain would be a stretch."

He looked sideways at her. "Thank you...I think."

"The question is what will Vance do with my

mother."

"You think he will harm her when he finds out his plans for escape are ruined?"

"I don't know. Actually, I was planning on rescuing her tonight."

Tanner dropped his glass, but she caught it before it fell to the floor. Only a small bit of wine caught the edge of her lace.

He took the glass back. "Stop joking with me."

"The townhouse is only a few streets away. I was going to slip out, break in, and take her to Agatha's, then come back here."

Tanner stared at her. "You're joking, right?"

"Think about it. Why else would I be carrying a loaded pistol in the pocket of my cloak tonight?"

Roxanne watched as he worked through the logic, and his amused face turned to one of amazement. "So that's why you had a pistol with you. But you couldn't have done it."

"Why not? It's the last thing anyone would expect."

"But a thousand things could go wrong."

"Vance is here now. He can't stop me. You engage him in conversation and I'll go get Mother." As she moved away, Tanner grabbed her arm.

"You've already discharged your pistol, so you can't possibly attempt the rescue tonight. He must have guards in the town house. By tomorrow there will be a warrant for Vance's arrest."

"That won't make Mother safe. It will simply make Vance more desperate. And she can be held hostage as well."

"I am charged with getting Holly and you safely home again tonight. Please promise me that you won't then crawl down the ivy and go to your brother's townhouse in the wee hours."

"I'm surprised at you, Tanner. If you were at all observant, you would realize my aunt's house has no ivy."

"Rox, please."

"Oh, very well. I promise not to attempt Mother's escape at night. It could be more dangerous."

"I should say so. You relieve my mind. You see how well we just worked together? You don't have to face these dragons alone."

"You now know what it feels like to have someone you love in danger, so don't blame me for being anxious."

"Your mother has kept him at bay for three years. I think you should trust her competence just as I am learning to trust yours."

"But we don't know what that has cost her. I don't want her in his power a moment longer than necessary."

"Tomorrow Vance will be arrested. If not, I will storm the gates of that castle for you."

Chapter Fifteen

"They ruined the casting," Tanner said when Fredrick was admitted to his house early the next morning. Should you even be up?"

Fredrick rubbed his forehead and shrugged. "Only to be expected on the first try. Might I inquire as to your intentions?"

Normally, Fredrick would have joined Tanner for breakfast or at least a cup of coffee. Instead he stood at attention by one of the breakfast parlor chairs, forcing Tanner to his feet.

"To try again."

"I meant with my sister."

"I asked Rox to marry me twice."

"Oh, without speaking to me first?"

Tanner tossed his napkin on the table. "We both know that would be useless. She turned me down. I want to be sure of my footing before I try again."

Fredrick relaxed his stance and gave Tanner a sad smile. "She's in love with you."

"So she says, but she's still distracted with what to do about your mother. She's convinced Vance murdered your father. Could that possibly be true?"

Fredrick sat down tiredly, and Tanner got him coffee and eggs from the sideboard.

"Now that I think of it, he was in the house that night. Rox said they had been drinking together. She never liked Vance. She said she heard the shot. Perhaps if I had been there… But I was at school."

"Then it is possible that he was murdered, as she believes. But by his best friend?"

"It was Vance who claimed that friendship. My impression was that father tolerated him."

"So how did he get all this power?"

"Our family solicitor. All the old man said was that Vance had been left our guardianship until we came of age."

"What about your mother?"

"She didn't seem happy about it, but she did not dispute it. I should not have gone back to school, but what could I have done? I had no power to act."

"According to Rox, your birthday is today. Perhaps you should visit this solicitor."

"Oh, I found out he died last year, but the firm is still there. Yes, I made an appointment."

"Do you want me to come with you?"

"I think I can handle it."

"So you don't want me to act in this matter?"

"If you get involved, you may make Rox angry. Of course, she would rather believe Father was murdered than that he committed suicide. I would myself. But where's the proof?"

"Rox says she has proof, the forged will."

"I am on my way there now." Fredrick drained his cup and pushed himself up out of the chair.

"May I be of any help? I hate just sitting here and waiting."

"Not unless you enjoy being bored for hours over legal matters. I do wish you would speak to Rox. You were as instrumental in saving our lives as Harding."

"I wish that were true." Tanner paced in front of his desk. "Yes, I must go to her to keep her from staging a rescue of your parent in broad daylight. She is convinced Vance means to snatch her away again."

"Harding indicated Vance would be arrested if Stone informed against him. And the yacht is being held, so he can't exactly just sail away. Rox says Fenster is getting a warrant for Vance's arrest anyway."

"I wait only for Harding's visit before I go to treat with Rox again."

****

"Miss Whitcomb," Fenster said. "I was expecting your brother."

"He was abducted last night and nearly killed. He does plan to keep his appointment this morning, but I just thought to look in and update you."

"Abducted?"

"By Vance's agent. By the way, have you run down your missing clerk yet?"

"No, and he absconded with my ready cash. I trusted him just because he always worked for Father."

"Apparently he could be bought."

"Since you are here, I can give you a précis of the situation, but your brother must come and sign the papers before his capital can be put at his disposal. Though I hope he does not mean to touch that. The interest should provide enough of a living."

"Only *his* capital."

"Yes, yours will be held in trust for two more years. I did a thorough search and found the original documents, not the ones Vance forged. My clerk must have been hanging on to them for a spot of blackmail against Vance later. Your brother will be your guardian."

"Very well."

"He should clear five thousand a year as well."

"And my mother?"

"The same."

"So we have been living on cabbage soup and darning our socks while Vance enjoyed our money."

"That is how I see it, but the bulk of the fortune is intact. Things could be much worse."

"My father is dead because of Vance. That's as bad as it gets. No, I should not say that. Fredrick could have been killed too. Who knows what was planned for my friend Holly, and all because she visited here with me. It was unwise of me to involve her."

Suddenly Roxanne felt overwhelmed by the danger she had put them all in. She'd dragged Holly into her affairs without stopping to think Vance might revenge himself on her for Tanner's attack on Stone and for her own interference in his plans. The clerk was obviously working for Vance and must have told him the jig was up. Hence the kidnapping. No doubt he planned to dispose of Roxanne and her mother at some point also, perhaps in the Channel.

"Miss Whitcomb, you look so pale. Are you well enough to see yourself home? Let me call you a hackney."

"My maid waits below. Actually that would be very kind of you. But it just occurred to me that you and your family might be in danger."

"I have not yet married, and I have already filed a complaint with the magistrate, so it would do Vance no good to kill me."

"It wouldn't do you a lot of good, either. Last night we had his cousin arrested. If Vance knows that, he will become more desperate."

"He is crippled now, I tell you. I've notified the exchange that he is no longer empowered to act on behalf of your brother. Besides, today is Fredrick's birthday anyway."

"So Vance won't be able to sell out of the funds and carry our money off to France?"

"No. Everything is perfectly safe now."

"How I wish that to be true. I'm sure my brother will be along directly. I still have to rescue my mother from Vance."

"Should you be attempting that alone?"

"I fear leaving it any longer."

Though she needed no assistance and just wanted to get away as soon as possible, Roxanne let herself be helped down the stairs by Mr. Fenster and got into the hackney his youngish new clerk had ordered for her. He had asked her a multitude of questions, and she was almost afraid he would insist on coming with her. But she did not want to put anyone else in danger from Vance. During the brief ride with her maid, Roxanne's mind still churned over the night's events.

They had been received if not warmly, at the ball, at least with no more than the usual amount of coldness. There were some whispers behind fans, but the words she caught were "horse" and "galloping," not "abduction" and "shooting." Such a small mercy.

How odd that her biggest fear yesterday was dwarfed by comparison with what had occurred last night. Was Fenster right? Was all this almost over? They had enough samples of her father's signature to prove the new will a forgery, but that didn't bring home a charge of murder on Vance. And while he lived, he was her mother's husband. Perhaps she could provoke a confession out of him in front of a witness. He seemed the sort to boast of his conquests. But how to contrive it?

And then there was the clerk, Goff. She had forgotten about him last night. By now he might have apprised Vance of the situation. The man could be even now spiriting her mother away. She must make all haste to get home, collect what she required, and not wait for any help. Even if she could not defeat Vance, she could at least delay him.

****

Tanner received Harding in his home office with as much trepidation as he had when he'd interviewed other applicants for Holly's hand. "I think I know what you wish to speak to me about."

Harding held his uniform hat tucked under his left arm. "So formal after last night. A blind man would have known I was in love with Holly all these months, yet you never considered the possibility I might be worth more to her than any of these fops."

Since Harding stood at attention, Tanner did not take a seat either. "Your condemnation is just. You saved her life. I can hardly refuse to let you marry her. I should—"

"And yet it grates with you," Harding said coldly. "I will marry her whether I have your permission or not."

"I said I would be no impediment, but she isn't of age. There are documents to be signed. Settlements."

"She needs the permission of a parent or guardian. We have her mother's permission. We don't need yours. We don't need you, Tanner. I can take care of her myself. I will come for her when all is arranged. It might not be a grand expensive wedding, but our marriage will have nothing to do with money and all to do with love."

Harding spun on his heel and left him gaping. The man did not expect or even want any of Holly's money. Why was that such a shock? If Rox had taught Tanner nothing else, it should be that money does not drive people the way it does business. Not all people, anyway. His problem was that he had dealt only with shallow people or that they had not revealed to him any depth. He'd considered Holly and his mother exceptions until he'd met Rox, Fredrick, and Harding.

Tanner sat for a moment trying to think of a way to redeem himself, and he could not. Perhaps in time Holly, Harding, and Roxanne would forgive him, but would it be in time for him to have a future with his dear Rox? He was not at all sure about that.

"Spencer. Are you all right?"

He had not noticed his mother enter and did not know how to answer her. "No, I am a wreck." He leaned against the edge of the desk.

"It's not quite that bad. No one died."

"But they might have if not for Rox's guesswork. And every time she asked for my help I refused her." He stood up and paced to the window.

"You didn't refuse her last night." His mother seated herself on the edge of a wingback chair. "You threw yourself into what could have been a dangerous or embarrassing mess, and I have a feeling you enjoyed it."

"Yes, I did, once the uncertainty was over. There is nothing like it in the carefully planned world of business. But I have asked Rox to marry me several times, and something always gets in the way of her saying yes."

His mother smiled. "She loves you. That is apparent from the way her gaze follows you."

"But does she admire me? Does she think me worthy

of her?" He came to sit on the arm of the chair.

"I think so. She asked my advice about something last night."

"What was it? Or are you at liberty to say?"

"She wanted to know if I thought she could make you happy. I said yes, of course, that she was the only woman who could."

"She asked your permission to marry me? I never heard of such a thing before."

"She's an original."

"Very true. But what am I? Because I have money I think I have power, but I have done nothing of any use. Look at Rox, penniless and she has managed all."

"I think she understands what real power is."

"What is that?"

"Love. It makes all things possible."

"She once told me she didn't think she was cut out for love."

"That's because she always sacrifices her own feelings for those she loves. The man who wins her will have a prize beyond price."

"She can't possibly love me. I dragged my feet at every turn in this mess."

"Not when it really counted."

"I doubted her until I saw her brother on that ship. Then my heart did stop, for I knew Holly must be there as well."

"Holly seems to have survived the experience. Did you notice how animated she was last evening? Agatha told me that several young gentlemen were taken with her, now that it is too late for them."

"Yes, that is how I imagined she would feel for her come-out, joyful and lively. Why the change? Is it the relief of not being killed?"

"It is the surety of Harding's love and her marriage to him."

"Shall we give them a house for a present? It will have to come from you, since he wants nothing from me."

"I don't think he will accept that."

"Perhaps his own ship, then. I shall think of something."

"Roxanne can't give a thought to her own happiness so long as her brother is in danger. Today is his birthday but that does not make him safe. If Vance has him killed even now, he might still get away with his scheme."

"I must go to Rox and help her even if I get arrested for breaking into her brother's house."

Chapter Sixteen

Harding called at Manchester Square and found Roxanne with her cloak over her arm just ready to depart. He reported that the kidnapping and smuggling affair had turned into a feather in his cap. Holly had accepted his proposal and had begun packing but felt saddened that he and his ship were being called back to duty. The marriage would occur three weeks after he returned to Exeter. He had been promised three days' leave for the event. Their family was invited, if they wished to attend.

"Wild horses could not keep us away," Roxanne said as she drew on her gloves. "We will all come. What about Tanner?"

"He isn't throwing any obstacles in our path, but I don't think he likes the idea much."

"After last night? Perhaps you misread him. He owes you his sister's life."

"And he owes you his. Stone was going to kill him. It strikes me Tanner is not the sort who likes to owe debts, not ones he can't discharge with money."

"I'm sure he'll come around," she said with her usual confidence. "Look how much progress he has made."

"I will always be prepared to accept his friendship if he is willing to offer it." Harding picked up his hat and turned to go.

"He needs time to think...and possibly just one

more scare."

Harding twitched his head in her direction. "Now you're worrying me. What do you have in mind?"

"It would be easier for Holly to arrange her new life with you if she is nearby. I was going to invite her to stay with Mother and me at the carriage house at Whitcomb Hall, with her mother's permission, of course. You'd be able to see her every day you are in port."

"Capital, but why not stay at the Hall?"

It was a question Roxanne had asked herself, and she thought she finally knew the answer. "That's where my father died. I don't think I can stay there until he has been avenged." She could see Harding's eyes open wide.

"By you?" Harding sounded truly worried now.

"No, silly. What could I possibly do? Just come and visit us there in few days' time."

"I see. And no one is going to let Tanner know where you have gone?"

"It's just a thought."

"I like your plan, and I suppose Tanner deserves to be worried at least once more."

Roxanne waited for Harding to go down the steps. He was happy and so was Holly. The one thing she could not bear was for him to be killed or injured, now that their future was assured. She couldn't ask him to spend any of his last few hours in London fighting her battle.

It did occur to her that she should wait for Tanner, give him a chance to prove himself. But what if he was killed by Vance? She would lose him. Holly and her mother would be devastated. It would put an end to all Fredrick's plans. No, she must not risk Tanner either, even though she had made a promise to him.

There was only one person left to free her mother.

She really needed a plan, for she would have to rescue her mother on her own.

She had barely seen Harding off when a note arrived from Vance that confirmed her decision. It said they were packing to return to the continent. This would be her last chance to see her mother before the ship departed. That must mean he did not yet know that Harding's crew had captured the yacht. Of course it was a trap, but at least she would be admitted. If she didn't go, there was no telling what Vance would do to her mother when he discovered he was no longer in possession of the *Silverloo* or any of the resources of their fortune.

The most important thing about the note was that it gave her permission to do as she wanted—to go after her mother herself. But she needed to take precautions in case something went wrong. Roxanne wrote a letter to her brother and had a footman carry it to the solicitor's office. Fredrick would be closeted with him for hours, so he was sure to be there.

She also penned a note to Tanner, outlining her plan, even though she had no right to demand anything from him. She didn't want to risk him, but it seemed unfair to deny him the chance to ride in on his charger. She dispatched the other footman with that letter. She just hoped to have the situation in hand before he arrived.

After some thought, Roxanne put the pistol in her largest reticule and a pen knife in her half boot. She'd worn an old brown dress in case there would be blood.

Roxanne admired the fine summer day as she walked the short distance to the town house. How could everything appear so calm when something desperate was about to happen? The fact that she was the one who was going to provoke the desperate situation seemed to calm her. Control was a heady intoxicant, even when it was an illusion.

She was admitted by a footman with a French accent. The man was surprised when she addressed him in French. Vance was waiting for her in the drawing room on the second floor, standing by the window, possibly having watched her approach like a predator waiting for a mouse to slip into his trap.

"You bid me come to say goodbye. Where is Mother?"

"I fear she is not well enough to see you."

Roxanne pulled off her gloves. "Then she can't be well enough to travel. Have you sent for the doctor?"

Vance stared at her.

"Or have you killed her?"

"Your mother is resting."

"Then why command me to come here?"

"I notified you. I am not required to do any more. My business here is concluded, and we plan to reside in France. The estate will be sold at auction. I had some thought that you might as well come with us, since you are ruined in London."

"How delightful. Let me run home and pack."

She moved toward the door, and Vance strode across the room to bar her way. "No need. We will buy you everything you need in Paris."

"But I must say goodbye to Fredrick and my aunt."

Roxanne was reaching the limits of how long she could delay this monster. She really began to fear her mother was dead.

"You may write to them."

"With the mail between Paris and England being so unreliable? I have not gotten one of Mother's letters and she none of mine."

"Servants can be so careless."

Roxanne smiled at Vance. She must not show any fear. "You can't have heard the latest on-dits."

"What possible interest could I have in London gossip?"

"That the *Silverloo* was captured for smuggling and impounded, and her erstwhile captain arrested."

Vance went pale. She was sure of it.

"I'm not responsible for the crew of the damned thing."

"They've been arrested without accomplishing their mission, which was to murder Fredrick and Holly."

"That's preposterous!" He strode to the window and looked out at the street as though expecting someone.

"Not according to Stone." She pulled the gun out and cocked it. "Leave now, without my mother, and you leave with your life, but you'll have to take the packet this time."

His face was scarlet with anger when he saw the gun in her hand. "You are presuming to dictate terms to me?"

"I'm not the only one who knows all your crimes and plots. Now Fenster the Younger suspects that you killed his father as well as mine."

Vance sneered at her. "I had nothing to do with his father's death."

"No, that was probably the clerk, Goff. Also, I told Fredrick everything."

"That is unfortunate." He advanced on her. "You have been far too busy."

"Fenster went to the magistrate days ago. There is a warrant for your arrest. If you know what is good for you, you will saddle a horse and ride away from

London."

"They have believed me all these years. No one will believe you. You're just a silly girl."

"I do not care what you think. I had rather not expose Mother to you any longer. So you have a choice, which is more than you gave Father. You can wait here to be arrested, flee to Europe without her, or take you own life. That is what is expected of a man who is ruined, isn't it?"

Vance snorted but kept his gaze on the pistol. "How ironic. I sold out of the funds before Waterloo and advised him to. If he had done what I did, he would have been ruined as well."

"But he might still be alive, and I would far rather have Father alive than have all the money in the world. Perhaps if you had been in the battle, instead of retired, you would have died with honor. But you came to the estate with the tragic news that all who sold out were ruined. Perhaps he laughed at you to reassure you because he believed our army would win. Is that when you shot him? Or did Stone bring more news later, that those who stayed in the funds were wealthy?"

He took another step in her direction, his hands fisting greedily as though he wanted her neck in their grasp. "Your imagination runs away with you."

"But mine does not," her mother said from the doorway. "I knew what you had done, but I thought I had no power to defeat you."

Her mother did not look as though she had been packing, for with her silk walking dress she was wearing a muff, a strange fashion accessory in such warm weather.

Vance stared in a puzzled way at her, then turned back to Roxanne. "You mean to shoot me in my own house?"

"No, I mean to shoot you in Fredrick's house."

"Rox, do you think you should?" her mother asked. "Would they call it self-defense?"

"I have considered the possibility of having to stand trial myself. But he won't flee to Europe as he should, or dispatch himself. What choice do I have?"

"How inconvenient for him, now that I have heard his confession also."

"I confessed nothing," Vance shouted.

"I heard him say he shot Father, didn't you?" Roxanne asked.

"I certainly did. Two witnesses should be enough."

"Good. We are leaving, Mother." She started backing toward the door.

"Will Fredrick be safe?"

"Yes, he is with the solicitor now."

Vance glared at her again, his gaze slicing the air between them.

"You've always known, haven't you?" Roxanne whispered.

"Yes. I knew the will was a forgery, but the old solicitor would not listen to me. I made a deal."

"And you became his prisoner."

"Better than being his wife."

Roxanne coldly looked Vance up and down. "A forced marriage is invalid. You are not his wife, so if he lives, you are still free."

"But is it safe to just let him go?" Her mother asked, pointing at him with her muff. "It seems he deserves some punishment. Possibly you could just wound him."

"Listen to you two, debating my future." Vance clenched his fists. "You're just a couple of women."

"You have to leave before the magistrate gets here, or you will be arrested." Roxanne moved so that she was closer to her mother's side rather than in front of her, for she had just remembered the significance of the muff.

Vance glanced toward the window. "I don't think there is anyone coming."

"Do you think I'd be stupid enough to come here alone if I didn't have a plan in motion?"

"Why did you come, you stupid girl?"

"You forget so quickly. You summoned me. But I needed to get Mother, and I came to convince you to leave and avoid scandal. You still have that opening, exile rather than death."

"Which is why I don't believe you. You'd never be satisfied with letting me go. You'd want revenge."

The arrival of a carriage in the street caused Vance to stride to the window, but he turned and smiled at them. For a horrible moment Roxanne thought Stone might have escaped. She listened to hasty steps on the stairs. If the man had been admitted, he was Vance's ally, not hers.

Goff paused breathless in the doorway a minute later.

"The jig's up! I goes to the ship like you said, but it's impounded. I nearly got arrested. 'Ow are we to get out of this now?"

"As always, by taking prisoners. You tie up my lady while I deal with the hellcat."

When Goff grabbed for her mother, Roxanne was startled by the shot, even though she had been expecting it. Goff spouted a blossom of scarlet on his side and keeled over. The muff pistol was a good ruse but one that was now spent.

While she was gawking, Vance grabbed her and

disarmed her, even as she heard an altercation at the street door, fists smacking skin, then a thunder of feet on the stairs. Tanner kicked the already open door wide and burst into the room with a pistol in his hand. Vance grabbed for her mother, but Roxanne put herself in his way so he held her father's pistol to her head.

"Let me out of here and I'll let her live."

"Just shoot him, Tanner. The gun isn't loaded."

"What?"

"Shoot him, I said. The pistol is empty."

"Who wants to find out?" Vance asked.

"No!" Tanner yelled and tossed his pistol aside.

Just then more footsteps on the stairs brought Fredrick into the doorway.

"You too, Fredrick," Vance ordered. "Toss your weapon aside or I will kill your sister."

"Certainly not. Father taught us all to shoot. I can hit you without endangering Roxanne in the slightest."

Tanner stared at him. "He's got a gun to her head. She's so self-sacrificing she might be willing to give up her life to save the two of you."

"I keep saying the pistol is not loaded. Why will no one believe me?"

"I believe her." Fredrick glared at Tanner. "Why don't you?"

"Because he's courageous enough to take a bullet to keep the rest of us safe," Roxanne said.

"Rox?" Tanner asked.

"Since I've got only one shot, who will it be? You, I think." Vance pointed the pistol at Tanner, who blew out a breath but kept his eyes open, staring at the barrel. Vance pulled the trigger, but there was only a harmless click.

Roxanne elbowed Vance in the stomach as she bent to retrieve her pen knife. But she had no need for it because Tanner took Vance down in a thunder of fists. She enjoyed every moment of watching Tanner beat the stuffing out of Vance.

Once Fredrick had tied up the semi-conscious Vance with a cord from the draperies, Tanner turned to her.

"You weren't lying. It wasn't loaded."

"It would be stupid of me to risk it. You got my note and came."

"What note?" Tanner still looked stunned.

"You came for me even though I didn't ask it of you?" She leaned toward him and kissed him, her arms reaching up to wrap themselves around his neck.

Fredrick laughed and came to hug his mother. "Yes, she would never risk letting him get his hands on a loaded gun."

"Actually, I was afraid that if I came here with a loaded pistol, he would goad me into murder."

"You're not capable of it," Tanner said.

"She did shoot Stone. Could have been a kill," Fredrick said as he walked to the window to investigate the sounds of yet another carriage.

Roxanne let go of Tanner to glare at her brother. "I should say not. I aimed to wound him and I did. Do these French servants seem unresponsive to so much noise?"

"I imagine they have all fled," her mother replied, "probably with the baggage."

The steps on the stairs this time heralded the arrival of the magistrate with Fenster.

"Which one is Vance?" the magistrate asked. Fenster pointed at Vance, who was awake enough to sit up but not stand.

"Captain Lucius Vance, I charge you in the name of the Crown with the murder of Sir Henry Whitcomb, extortion, embezzling, smuggling, and other summary offenses."

"I didn't. I don't care what they say. It was that clerk, Goff, who showed me the will. I thought it was genuine."

"So you are blaming Goff for everything?" Fenster asked as he gazed in a puzzled way at the wounded clerk, who was beginning to stir.

The magistrate stared down at the wound in Goff's side and the spill of blood onto the rug. "If he lives, he will stand trial with you."

They had almost forgotten the clerk and whether he was dead or not until his arm shot out with a pistol in it. "I'll not swing alone." He fired point blank at Vance and got him in the chest. The look of surprise on her torturer's face would give Roxanne nightmares for some time. Had her father been surprised when his army friend suddenly shot him?

She felt her knees grow weak and Tanner's strong arms supporting her as he guided her to a sofa. She was aware of Fredrick embracing her mother and casting the muff aside.

The magistrate shook his head. "This will complicate matters."

"Who shot the clerk?" Fredrick asked.

"Probably Vance," Fenster said. "Is Goff dead?"

"Not quite," said the magistrate. "I'll have them hauled away, then work on my report."

"We should be able to get a confession from Ian Stone now," Fredrick suggested.

"Rox?" Tanner asked.

She gazed up at Tanner and gave him a look that

should have melted him into a puddle. Then she withdrew to a corner of the sofa with tears in her eyes. "You came without my asking."

"Of course. I meant to have it out with Vance. I'm just sorry I was detained so long. There's a carriage in the stable yard loaded with baggage. If you had not arrived when you did, he might have abducted your mother again."

"But you thought the gun was loaded and tried to draw the fire to yourself. You are a hero, but you didn't believe me."

Tanner smiled weakly. "I trust your judgment, not your veracity."

He smiled at her, but she still felt breathless, as though she had been running a long race and only just finished.

"There's time now for us," she said. "The worst is over and we can all return to a normal life."

"Whatever that is to be. Is this a bad time to discuss our future?" he asked.

"The past is too much with me at the moment. Seeing Vance shot brings back memories of Father's murder. We must go to Aunt Agatha's house. I need a few hours."

Chapter Seventeen

Tanner walked into the breakfast parlor, pulling on his driving gloves and carrying a small valise. "I shall be gone the rest of the day, possibly tomorrow as well," he told his mother. He kept his gaze out the window on the fine day so at odds with his mood.

"Checking on the wool mill?" She dropped her toast on her plate and took a meditative sip of her tea.

"Possibly."

"If you are looking for Roxanne, best fortify yourself with a meal."

"How did you know that?" He poured himself a cup of coffee and drank it standing while he mused on her smug look.

"You love her. How could I not know it? Give her this ring." She put her cup down and drew a sapphire off her finger and handed it to him. "I hope it brings her more happiness than it did me."

"Your wedding ring." He smiled in spite of his worry. "Shall I consider this your blessing on the match if I can make it?"

"She'll understand, even if you don't."

As he left the room, he heard his mother mumble, "Young fool." And she was right. How could he have let Roxanne go without some sort of promise to wed? But she'd said she needed time, and only a villain would have pressed her when she had so much to discuss with her mother. Not to mention all that blood on the carpet. It simply wasn't the right moment. It never was for them. But he had expected her to stay at her aunt's town house.

Now Holly was missing, too, and he could only hope they were together and safe. He could not confess to his mother that he had mislaid his sister yet again. He had planned to beg Holly's maid to say she had a cold and his mother should stay away from her. But her maid was nowhere to be found either.

It never entered his head that Harding might have eloped with Holly. Captain Harding was a man of honor. But perhaps Holly had run to him. Tanner was setting a course for Exeter with all speed, hoping to find her before his mother went into a decline. He could send an express rider as soon as he had good news. With frequent changes of teams, he thought he could accomplish the trip in two days rather than three.

Before he left town, he stopped at the foundry and was not surprised to find Fredrick there.

"The new casting worked. We are one step closer to our compact steam engine."

"Good, good. I put you in charge here."

"Where are you going?" Fredrick wiped his hands on his pocket handkerchief.

"Both Holly and Rox are missing now."

"I'll go with you. Your men are competent to handle the cooling process."

"But you don't know where I'm going."

"Neither do you. A smart man would ask himself where Rox would retreat to."

"Whitcomb Hall?"

"Exactly."

Tanner might have enjoyed the two-day drive from

London if it had not been wracked with such suspense. It did not help that Fredrick drove part of the way, since it allowed Tanner to focus on the possible death of all his plans. When had he become so desperate? Before the appearance of Rox, he could take or leave women. Like Fredrick, his joy and passion had been work.

Now he didn't much care if the business foundered, except for Fredrick's engine. He had some fears in that respect, that an engine compact enough to run a wagon might for all its economy still be too dear for shepherds or draymen to afford, but someday it would come into its own.

Fredrick was driving when they crossed a bridge over the Exe River and turned up a short lane to a gatehouse. Holly and Lady Whitcomb waved to them through the window. Fredrick went to stable the horses while Tanner sought out the object of his desire, Roxanne. How odd that he had stopped fretting over Holly as soon as he knew her location, but that his concern for Rox had mounted with each mile.

He saw a figure in white muslin moving about in the garden, the strings of her wide-brimmed sun hat trailing behind her. Picking beans was an occupation that seemed to fit with what he had learned of her. He walked up behind her and took the basket. "I feel lucky to find you finally."

She turned to him with her sad smile, holding her sun hat on her head. "I don't believe in luck."

An argument already. He could only laugh at her refutation. "Very well, I asked your brother where you would be, and he was right."

"Good fortune must be earned." She pulled another handful of beans and dropped them into the basket. He took that as agreement that he might stay.

After they got to the end of the row, she walked toward the trellis and bench that marked the entrance to the kitchen garden and sat in the shade of the climbing roses. He wondered why the setting looked so familiar. Then he realized it was not unlike the bench he'd destroyed at Vauxhall defending her from Ian Stone. He'd been in love with her ever since. He sat beside her, but she took the basket and placed it between them.

"I agree. Fortune should not be inherited, but deserved. In some ways, I am no better than the idle aristocrats who treat their tenant farmers like slaves."

"They are not all like that anymore. And not all men of business care only about money. The world is a strange mix of people."

"I let you down. I never believed in your conspiracy until it was almost too late." Tanner watched those long dark lashes draw down over her blue-green eyes as she began shelling beans.

She shrugged and cast him a glance.

"You are not singular in that respect. Everyone I know has let me down at one time or another, and some have betrayed me past repair. With the exception of Fredrick and Holly. Harding has been a faithful friend as well. Why can you not give him and Holly your blessing? Let them be happy even if you cannot?"

Tanner laughed. "Is that your final term for winning you, that I should approve their marriage?" The scent of the roses was intoxicating and he wondered if that was why she had sat down here.

"It is somehow tied to my own happiness. I love you, Tanner, but I want to think well of you besides that. I admire you in all other things."

"I would have gladly given my consent, had Captain Harding not stormed out of my house informing me that they didn't need it, nor any of my money or Holly's."

"Perhaps he thought you were trying to buy his allegiance. I cared too much about you to let you buy me. I could have stood it with anyone else." She blinked and looked away. "No, that's not true. Once I met you, a love match with anyone else was unthinkable."

"But you are a woman who prizes equality. Should he not have consulted Holly before he whistled her fortune down the wind?"

"Yes, marriage should be a partnership, not one person taking care of another, but a reciprocal arrangement."

"Guilty on all counts. I tried to buy you with security. I thought I was doing the right thing. But I'm not a hero after all. No white knight, certainly. I make mistakes. Why do you think that is? Have you a theory about it?" He laughed a little in a desperate sort of way.

"I have been thinking of little else these past two days. It is because you are human but you won't admit it. You think you know what is best for everyone, and you act on that without consulting them."

"Guilty as charged."

Roxanne finally looked at him. "Of course, I do the same thing."

He tried to repress his smile. She was being serious, and he did not want to mock her. "Dare I agree with you?"

"I suppose you are here to take Holly back. Well, don't expect her to be the compliant child whose life you almost ruined. It was only to make you happy that she almost stepped into the trap you set for her. She's now made of stronger stuff and will not bow to your demands."

"And you've only had her under your wing a few weeks. I will not ask her to leave. What impulse made you bring her here?"

"She begged to come with me, away from London. I guess it was the same impulse that led me to follow her as she cried her way out of her own ball. No one should be that unhappy."

"And yet you were unhappy and never complained of it. But without telling anyone where you were going?"

Roxanne snapped her gaze back toward him. "What are you talking about? Fredrick knew. And your mother agreed."

"Mother knew?"

"Of course. She didn't tell you?"

He rubbed his forehead. "I didn't ask. I was hoping to find Holly before I had to confess to Mother that my stupidity had forced her to run away. Mother's health only just recovered from the abduction. I was afraid to break the news."

"Well, if that isn't the most craven…"

He stopped her breath with a kiss. When he paused, she stared at him, her eyes brimming with tears.

"I just wanted to do that since I can't seem to say anything right. What, no criticism of my kiss? Give me your worst review."

"It was too short," she said breathlessly.

He swept her into his arms and kissed her thoroughly, aware in the back of his mind that they could be observed from either the gatehouse or the main road. Then he looked at her. It seemed so perfect now, the two of them in this rose-scented bower.

"What now? Shall we argue some more?"

"I don't know what happens now," she said from the nest of his arms. "I've never gotten this close to love before. It's almost frightening."

"Is that why you drew back from me? Because you were afraid I might ruin it?"

"Yes. So long as we were just friends, you had not yet betrayed me and I had not done that to you either. It seemed the safer course."

"I'm no expert, but it strikes me that there is nothing safe about love. To give in to it means we must accept our hearts will be broken once in a while."

Rox smiled through her tears. "But mended again after much apology."

"I'm not saying I'll never make another mistake, but I want you to tell me when I do."

"Never fear. I will not let the slightest error pass without comment."

He glanced toward the gatehouse and released her. "Can you forgive me for accusing you of the baseness that was mine, seeking money rather than love?"

"I couldn't do it, marry you for your money. And when I realized that, I found I couldn't give such false allegiance to any other man, even Sir John Marbrey, whom I genuinely like. Is there nothing I can do for him now that he realizes he is ruined?"

"I can see he keeps his estate. Perhaps by paying exorbitant prices for all those horses you love so dearly? Or perhaps I need a right of way across his land. Why do you care for him so much? His son was only trying to get your inheritance. Were we the only ones in London ignorant of your fortune?"

"Possibly, since we don't listen to gossip. I feel for

Sir John because he was so deceived. He trusted his son and daughter-in-law and they betrayed him. Everyone he knew betrayed him."

"And you have much experience of that."

"Yes. At one point I even thought my mother betrayed me. Besides, he is a dear man."

"But not one you wish to marry?"

"It seemed like an easy choice when I didn't love anyone else."

"But now you do." He picked up one of her hands and entwined his fingers with hers.

"Yes, love changes everything. It makes you refuse to settle for less that the perfect life."

"What is your perfect life?" He turned her face up to look at him and tossed her sun hat out into the bean patch. It sailed away from them like a delicate bird.

"You, silly." Roxanne kissed him again. "You are my perfect life. If I can't marry you, I won't marry at all."

"But that is what I want, to marry you. It's what I've wanted all along."

"Even when I caused you so many problems?"

"More than ever then." He released her hands and stroked her cheeks with his fingers.

"Even after we fought, you came to rescue me, and without my even asking."

"I wasn't very good at it," Tanner confessed. "I didn't believe you when you said not to fear the pistol."

"You had only seen it fired, not misfired. Did you really think I would confront Vance with a loaded pistol? Nothing could be sillier."

"I should have guessed you would be sensible. So we have taken care of all, and we too are to have a happy ending? Could I have asked you to marry me that first night and saved us all this bother?"

Roxanne raised her chin to look at him. "No, because you were arrogant. Charming but too sure of yourself. And I did want Fredrick to succeed on his own."

"You wanted nothing for yourself."

"When you think you are responsible for your father's suicide, you don't think you are entitled to a life."

"Oh, Rox, who made you think that?" His hands slid down her shoulders to her waist and he gave her a warm hug.

"I thought of it myself. It was easier to blame me than Father or Mother. Once I introduced you and Fredrick, I could not interfere in his success."

"Still you refused me when Fredrick's future was secured."

"By then I feared for his life and Mother's. I could not think of myself. But really, it all hinged on how you treated Holly. If you had refused to let her find happiness with Captain Harding, it would have cast a shadow over my love for you."

He ran a finger along her determined chin. "I have been well instructed in empathy from you, not to mention humiliation. I have no pride left or confidence in my judgment."

"And I never had any pride or confidence, so we are free to be ourselves."

"I was trying to be something I was never meant to be. And I dragged my sister along resisting."

"I was trying to do something my conscience would not allow."

"Are we done with pretense, then?" he asked as he tugged at a lock of her hair.

"Yes. Look." Roxanne pointed toward the river. "Holly and Harding walking out along the tow path. Don't they look perfect together?"

He rose and pulled Rox to her feet. "They may be perfect, but we are who we are with all our faults and mistakes."

"And we care not a whit what the rest of the world thinks."

"Not a whit." He swept her into another kiss, ignoring the faces of her mother and brother at the window smiling at them.

A word about the author...

Barbara Jean Miller has mentored in the Writing Popular Fiction Masters Program at Seton Hill University since its inception in 1999.

She writes in several genres but her favorite is historical romantic suspense. She calls them action/adventure romances with the heroine sharing in the struggles and rescue in equal part with the hero. These struggles often involve mysteries and horses.

Barb lives with her husband and pets on an ancient farm in Western Pennsylvania, which contributes authentic settings to her novels.

https://barbarajeanmiller.substack.com

Thank you for purchasing
this publication of The Wild Rose Press, Inc.

For questions or more information
contact us at
info@thewildrosepress.com.

The Wild Rose Press, Inc.